DISSONANT HARMONIES

BEV VINCENT
BRIAN KEENE

CEMETERY DANCE PUBLICATIONS

CEMETERY DANCE PUBLICATIONS

'Dissonant Harmonies' © 2021 Bev Vincent, Brian Keene
'The Dead of Winter' © 2021 Bev Vincent
'The Motel at the End of the World' © 2021 Brian Keene

This is a work of collected fiction. All characters depicted in this book are fictitious, and any resemblance to actual events or persons, living or dead, is purely coincidental.

All rights reserved. No part of this book may be reproduced in whole or in part without the publisher's written consent, except for the purpose of review.

Artwork by Don Noble

Trade Paperback Edition

ISBN: 978-1-58767-803-5

www.cemeterydance.com

Acknowledgements

Both authors would like to thank Richard Chizmar, Brian Freeman, and everyone else at Cemetery Dance, Tod Clark, and Geoff Cooper for the title suggestion.

Bev Vincent would like to thank Tod Clark and Norman Prentiss for helpful suggestions about the first draft of the manuscript, and his wife Mary Anne. She's my #1 fan and I'm hers.

Brian Keene would like to thank Tod Clark, Mary SanGiovanni and my sons.

Table of Contents

The Mix Tapes: An Introduction	7
The Dead of Winter – Bev Vincent	25
Story Notes – Bev Vincent	127
The Motel at the End of the World – Brian Keene	129
Story Notes – Brian Keene	157
Author Bios	161

THE MIX TAPES:
AN INTRODUCTION

Bev Vincent and Brian Keene

BACK IN 2007, we observed (via Twitter) that we both write to music, and that we listened to some of the same music while writing—but not all. We decided to explore how music might influence our writing differently.

The idea never fell completely off our radars, but other obligations pushed it to the back burner. The concept morphed, too. Originally, we thought we would write a "concept album" of short stories but eventually decided we would each create a playlist for the other person to listen to exclusively while working on a novella.

Bev originally dubbed it "The Pink Floyd Effect" because it reminded him of The Alan Parsons Project, and was thus a nod to two of our mutual favorites. Six years later, when Bev suggested the title to Brian, Brian paused for a long second and then said, "How attached are you to that?" And, thus, this book bears a different title!

Anyway, the idea was simple. Given that we both usually write to music, we'd make each other a mix tape or playlist. Each of us would then listen to that playlist and wait for inspiration to strike. When it did, we would only listen to that playlist while working on the two stories included in this book. Thus, Bev's novella, *The Dead of Winter*, was inspired and fueled solely by Brian's playlist, and Brian's novella, *The Motel at the End of the World*, was solely inspired and fueled by Bev's playlist.

The concept of the "mix tape" wasn't completely alien to Bev, but he was more of an AOR guy. He doesn't buy singles—he buys albums. He never uses the shuffle feature on his iPod—he listens to records from start to finish. But he does remember creating tapes of favorite songs borrowed from friends while in university.

BEV VINCENT & BRIAN KEENE

Brian was a mix tape enthusiast, having made countless tapes in the late-Seventies and early-Eighties (mostly for girls he was dating, or hoping to date, but occasionally for friends who he wanted to turn on to a then-new band like Iron Maiden or Prince or Run-DMC). He always has Spotify on shuffle, but like Bev, he also enjoys listening to albums from beginning to end.

Having gone through the process of choosing one CD's worth of music, we both now have much greater sympathy for musical groups who have to a) pick which songs to use on an album and which ones to leave behind, and b) decide on the best running order. The problem is something akin to what anthology and collection editors face. There needs to be a logical sequence and a flow. We both spent considerable time agonizing over this.

Here's what we ended up sending to each other.

BEV'S MIX TAPE FOR BRIAN

Track 1: Dead Man's Blues by Supertramp (album: *Slow Motion*)

BEV: The first rock concert I ever attended was during Supertramp's Breakfast in Canada tour in 1979. I'd become hooked on the group a couple of years earlier after buying *Even in the Quietest Moments* based solely on the album cover, which features a snow-covered piano atop a mountain and sheet music labeled "Fool's Overture" on the rack that is actually the score for "The Star-Spangled Banner." It would

DISSONANT HARMONIES

have been a no-brainer to include "Fool's Overture," which is high on my list of favorite songs. However, I decided to pick something Brian might be less familiar with. I love the horn solos on this one, and the title seemed ideal for this project.

BRIAN: Supertramp's *Breakfast in America* is my fourth favorite album of all time (edged out only by Prince's *Purple Rain*, Faith No More's *Angel Dust*, and Queensryche's *Operation: Mindcrime*. It's also one of the first albums I ever purchased as a kid, and I still own that copy over forty years later. But Bev was correct in assuming that I wouldn't be as familiar with "Dead Man's Blues". I don't think I'd ever heard this deep cut before Bev put it on the playlist, but it was the essential driver behind the idea for my story. (For more on that, I'll refer you to the story notes at the end).

Track 2: Mount Teidi by Mike Oldfield (album: *Five Miles Out*)

BEV: I could write entire novels listening only to Mike Oldfield. I think I have everything he's ever recorded, including most of the live performances. My favorite is the live debut recording of *Tubular Bells II* (called *The Sorcerer*). Most of what he does is instrumental, which is perfect for writing.

BRIAN: I wasn't familiar with Mike Oldfield at all, with the exception of the theme from *The Exorcist*. Bev's correct in that the instrumental stuff is great for writing.

Track 3: Nothing Is Something Worth Doing by Shpongle (album: *Ineffable Mysteries from Shpongleland*)

BEV: On a recent album, *A Vital Path*, Alan Parsons collaborates with Simon Posford, who is half of the two-man team known as Shpongle. Their music is described as "trance," and I love listening to it while I write. The distinctive instrument on this song is called the hang drum. It looks like a wok and produces the most amazing sound. Find the live version performed at the Roundhouse in London on YouTube to see an incredible performance.

BRIAN: Another one I wasn't familiar with, but I am now a fan, and have written some other stuff with Shpongle on in the background.

BEV VINCENT & BRIAN KEENE

Track 4: Fortunate Son by Bruce Hornsby (album: *Spirit Trail*)

BEV: The lyrics cut like a knife, in much the same way as they did in Hornsby's earlier song, "The Way It Is." His piano-playing chops have me in awe, his vocals are amazing and his lyrics sophisticated. He is a master of improv, a skill probably cultivated during his touring days with The Grateful Dead in the late 80s and early 90s. I am particularly impressed by the way he never seems to play a song the same way twice. There's a live version of this song that segues into Pink Floyd's "Comfortably Numb," but it was too long.

BRIAN: I was a fan of this one long before Bev included it on his playlist. I was lucky enough to see Bruce Hornsby live while I was serving in the Navy. I still have fond memories of that fantastic show—one of many such live performances I was fortunate enough to see while serving. Others included Bob Dylan and Tom Petty in either Haifa or Tel Aviv (I can still remember the concert but not which city I saw it in), Bruce Springsteen in Los Angeles, Run-DMC and The Fat Boys in San Diego, and a ton of concerts at the Hampton Roads Coliseum near the Norfolk naval base—Van Halen, KISS, Wasp, Rush, Billy Idol, Til Tuesday, The Cult, and many more.

Track 5: Oxygène Part IV by Jean Michel Jarre (album: *Oxygène*)

BEV: Shortly before I moved to Texas, Jean Michel Jarre conducted a huge out-door concert in Houston where he projected lasers onto the sides of the downtown's skyscrapers. I'm sorry I missed that. This track is a throwback to the 1960s Moog synthesizer-based song "Popcorn."

BRIAN: I dug this one quite a bit. It reminded me in some ways of some of the stuff Joe Meek was doing in studio before his suicide. I always thought Joe Meek's story was ripe for a fictionalized horror novel, sort of like what people have done with the folklore surrounding Robert Johnson and the infamous crossroads. To the best of my knowledge, only Alan Moore has done such a thing, on his spoken word album *The Highbury Working* (in collaboration with Tim Perkins and Bauhaus's David J).

DISSONANT HARMONIES

Track 6: Crystalline Green by Goldfrapp (album: *Black Cherry*)

BEV: I don't remember where I first encountered Goldfrapp, but if hadn't heard of them already, I probably would have through the use of their song "Ooh La La" on an iPhone commercial. This is a beautiful track. Very moody. The album *Black Cherry* has several excellent songs.

BRIAN: Hadn't heard Goldfrapp before this but liked the song enough that I did some searching online, and recognized the song from the iPhone commercial!

Track 7: No Answers Only Questions by The Alan Parsons Project (album: *Vulture Culture*)

BEV: Alan Parsons had to be on this playlist, but which song? I love instrumentals like "The Gold Bug," "Mammagamma" and "Lucifer." Brian told me he hadn't listened to *Vulture Culture* in decades, which inspired me to include this previously unreleased song that appeared on the remastered version of the album. It features Eric Woolfson on vocals and the kind of existential lyrics that appeal to me.

BRIAN: I love The Alan Parsons Project. I mean, come on... they've made concept albums about Edgar Allan Poe, Isaac Asimov and the mysteries of the pyramids of Giza. Growing up, *The Turn of A Friendly Card*, *Eye In The Sky*, and *Ammonia Avenue* were always in heavy rotation in my bedroom. In fact, the first time I got high, it was to side one of *Eye In The Sky*. Sadly, with the exception of the opening track ("Let's Talk About Me") and the phenomenal "Days Are Numbers (The Traveler)", the rest of *Vulture Culture* never grabbed me the way those previous three albums did, and I hadn't listened to it in years. As a result, I never bothered with the reissues, which included this unreleased track. I'm glad Bev put it on here. My favorite of the mix, and a tune that heavily impacted my novella.

Track 8: I Hope I Never by Split Enz (album: *True Colours*)

BEV: Growing up in Canada, I was exposed to some different music than Brian was. In addition to the popular American music of the time and our own homegrown musicians, many of whom never crossed over to the US, there were all of the Commonwealth groups that were more popular in Canada than south of the border. Chris de Burgh, for example, was huge in Canada, but he's probably known for only one or two songs in the US. Even Supertramp had a larger following in Canada than in the States. Despite a couple of American tours, New Zealand's Split Enz never made it big here. This album was popular when it came out because the vinyl LP was laser etched. When you held it up to the light, you could see colored geometric shapes on the surface. Try that with an MP3. The Finn brothers wrote some dark songs (Check out "Charlie," for example), but this one is among the bluntest. Tell us how you really feel, Tim.

BRIAN: Yep! I can't say I was ever a huge fan of the Split Enz, but I had a friend who was, and I remember that laser-etched album. We were teenagers who spent hours examining the background minutia in the artwork of Iron Maiden's album covers, and turning our Dio records upside down (because his stylized logo spells out DEVIL when you do that), so yeah... that album was a trip. Oddly enough, I don't ever remember us actually listening to it. We'd just look at it, tilting it in the light, while we listened to Rush's *2112* or Pink Floyd's *Wish You Were Here* instead.

Track 9: People Are Like Suns by Crowded House (album: *Time on Earth*)

BEV: I like the word "segue," so this transition tickles my fancy. Crowded House was formed from the ashes of Split Enz and gained a wider international audience. You may be familiar with "Don't Dream It's Over" from *The Stand* soundtrack. This is the work of a more mature, introspective artist. And one who's a lot less pissed off.

BRIAN: A great song by a great band, and another junction where Bev's tastes and my tastes collide.

Track 10: I Can't Decide by Scissor Sisters (album: *Ta-Dah*)

BEV: Brian and I both have stories in the anthology *Doctor Who: Destination Prague*. I first heard this song played over a scene featuring the Master (John Simm) in the episode "The Last of the Time Lords" and was delighted by its saucy and jaunty tone. It seemed a perfect fit for the Master. I don't know what the hell the band was thinking when they wrote it, though.

DISSONANT HARMONIES

BRIAN: My introduction to Scissor Sisters was during my 2016 cross-country promotional tour for my novels *The Complex* and *Pressure*. I was driving from a signing in New Orleans to a signing in Florida, and I stopped for gas at a small, independently owned convenience store. The cashier had the radio cranked, and "I Don't Feel Like Dancing" was blasting from the speakers. It's an insanely infectious song that pays homage to the best disco and dance-pop of the seventies. If there's one thing I am unabashed about regarding music, it is my deep love of disco. I asked the cashier who the band was, paid for my purchase, hopped back in my rental car, and immediately began working my way through their catalogue of music.

Track 11: Wicked Dreams by Elton John (album: *The Big Picture*)

BEV: If there's any performer who has been a constant presence in my life, it's Elton John. His first greatest hits album was the first non K-Tel record I ever bought. My brother had to tell me to stop playing "Crocodile Rock" on one rainy afternoon. I saw Elton play for two and a half hours in front of 72,000 people at Wembley Stadium in London in 1984. I've seen him perform a number of times since, but that was the most memorable concert. "Funeral for a Friend" might have been the obvious choice, but I settled on "Wicked Dreams" because it is a rare rocker in his recent catalog, and its tone and lyrics seemed apropos. Turn it up to 11 and get writing!

BRIAN: Another example of our musical tastes merging. While Billy Joel will always and forever be my primary piano man, I am indeed a big fan of Elton John's, as well. "Wicked Dreams" is a great track—probably my favorite from his more recent catalog (although a close second would be the heartbreaking reworked version of "Rocket Man" that appeared in the television show *Californication*).

Track 12: Billy by Nik Kershaw (album: *15 Minutes*)

BEV: Kershaw was a pop sensation in the Commonwealth in the 1980s. He also performed at Wembley the day I saw Elton John, and I've followed his career ever since. His lyrics tend to be clever—puns or twists on popular sayings. I listened to "Billy" over and over when

I wrote a short story called "Missing Evvie," about an abusive relationship.

BRIAN: This artist was new to me. I liked it fine enough, but not sure I could write to him.

Track 13: Wait by Wang Chung (album: *Points on the Curve*)

BEV: Huh. I just realized that Wang Chung also played at that 1984 concert in Wembley. I guess it had a profound effect on me (but not enough to include Big Country, who also played that day). You may recognize this song from the William Friedkin movie *To Live and Die in L.A.*

BRIAN: I love Wang Chung. They were part of the soundtrack of my high school years. This is one of my favorites by them, from one of my favorite albums. Seriously, it's simply one of the best soundtracks of that era, and a crystalline, picture-perfect auditory snapshot of the music and style of that era.

Track 14: My Little Island by Mike + The Mechanics (album: *M6*)

BEV: The obligatory ballad, this song begins with the retro sound of a needle on vinyl. I saw Mike + The Mechanics at the Hallenstadion in Zurich when I lived there in the late 1980s. According to them, it was their first concert ever. One of their two lead singers (both named Paul) forgot the lyrics to some of the songs, so I guess that was true. Mike is, of course, Mike Rutherford from Genesis, and you're probably familiar with *The Living Years* and the hit singles from their debut album. This is more recent, a haunting little piece that I can put on repeat and listen to over and over again.

BRIAN: I'm a fan of Genesis, and I liked Mike + The Mechanics debut album, but I never really followed them after "The Living Years". After hearing this haunting, evocative ballad, I went out and corrected that.

Track 15: The Bridge by Elliott Brood (album: *Ambassador*)

BEV: Here's one I'm pretty sure Brian has never heard before. I could have run rampant with Canadiana. I reined in my patriotic tendencies, but I thought Brian would enjoy this one.

DISSONANT HARMONIES

Brood's musical style has been dubbed "death country." I listened to this album while driving across West Texas several years ago and it was perfect mood music, especially when I stopped at Langtry, former home of Judge Roy Bean, the law west of the Pecos.

BRIAN: Bev's right. I hadn't heard this before. But holy shit, I'm glad I've heard it now! One of my faves off the playlist, and "death country" suits it all too well.

Track 16: Julie Don't Live Here by Electric Light Orchestra (album: *Time*)

BEV: This one just makes me smile. It's from the remastered version of the album. Such a jaunty piece. How could they have left it off the original recording? Well, you could only fit 50 minutes on a vinyl album—if you held your breath and squeezed in the last few notes.

BRIAN: I've always been an E.L.O. fan, going back to childhood (*Discovery* was one of my first vinyl purchases). They've been experiencing something of a comeback in the Keene household as my eleven-year old son has discovered them via the usage of "Mr. Blue Sky" in an animated movie. As a result, he and I have been working our way through their entire discography.

Track 17: On the Turning Away by Pink Floyd (album: *A Momentary Lapse of Reason*)

BEV: Of course, there had to be a Floyd song, but there are so many to choose from. I could have gone obscure (I tormented my friends with *Umma Gumma* when I discovered Pink Floyd during my first year at university, the year *The Wall* came out), but I settled on this one, one of my favorites. I saw them at Rice Stadium in Houston during their *Division Bell* tour—it was the only time in their history that they had to cut short a concert because of rain. Their instruments kept shorting out. On the other hand, the laser effects were brilliant in the downpour.

BRIAN: I agree, there had to be a Floyd song, given the mood and tenor of the previous tracks Bev included. Admission, though—this particular track is my least favorite of the post-Waters singles. I would have picked "One Slip" maybe?

Track 18: Kiss Your Ass Goodbye by Styx (album: *Cyclorama*)

BEV: I'm half a dozen years older than Brian, so my school music was different from his. *Crystal Ball* and *The Grand Illusion* both came out when I was a teenager. Once I like a group, I become a completist, so I bought all their earlier albums, and kept up with them until 1990's *Edge of the Century*. Then they fell off my radar, for some reason, until I stumbled upon *Cyclorama*. I was delighted to discover that Gowan had become one of their lead singers. If you lived in Canada in the 1980s, you knew Gowan from songs like "Strange Animal" and "Criminal Mind." This song pumps me up every time I hear it. What better note on which to end the CD?

BRIAN: I mentioned E.L.O.'s *Discovery* being one of the first albums I ever bought. The very first album was Styx's *The Grand Illusion*. I guess I must have been eight or nine years old? I brought it home and spent an entire weekend in my room, reading comic books and just playing the album over and over and over again. I was a fan and remain a fan—even to the point of defending *Kilroy Was Here* when everyone else was disowning the band for it—but like Bev, they fell off my radar after the pop schmaltz of *Edge of the Century*. I, too, rediscovered them with *Cyclorama*. This is a great track. If you dig it, also check out their cover of "I Am The Walrus", which I believe was recorded around the same time?

B-SIDES

BEV: These artists didn't make the final cut, as much as I wanted to include them:

- Jon and Vangelis. I love "The Friends of Mr. Cairo," which is inspired by many of the great noir films, but it's way too long, so it had to go.
- Emerson, Lake and Palmer. I wanted to include Emerson's piano concerto from his side of the *Works Volume 1* album (the black one), but it runs nearly 20 minutes. Terrific writing music.

DISSONANT HARMONIES

- Fountains of Wayne. Some day I'd like to write a cycle of short stories, each one inspired by a different FoW song. So many of them are complete little tales or vignettes.
- The Buggles. If you ever want a 1980s flashback, search "Buggles live" on YouTube and watch the two videos from the 2004 Prince's Trust concert where they perform their two most famous songs, "Video Killed the Radio Star" and "Living in the Plastic Age."
- Warren Zevon. I wanted to include "Mr. Bad Example" because, well, it's Zevon, but also because it was the inspiration for my story "Wake Me Up For Meals," which appeared in *Ellery Queen's Mystery Magazine*. I had the rare pleasure of seeing Zevon perform with the Rock Bottom Remainders at the Miami Book Fair in 1997. Cool dude.
- Kansas. I can't believe I didn't include something from them. "Cheyenne Anthem," for example.

BRIAN'S MIX TAPE FOR BEV

Track 1: Shut Up, Be Happy by Ice-T (album: *The Iceberg/ Freedom of Speech*)

BRIAN: These days, everyone knows Ice-T as the actor who plays a cop on *Law & Order: SVU*. Or maybe they remember him as one of the most influential rappers of all time. Fewer people know him as the lead singer of the heavy metal band Body Count, and even less realize that both metal and horror have always played a role in his upbringing and his music. From the sampling of the Halloween theme on "The

Tower" (from the seminal album *O.G. Original Gangster*) to displaying *Phantasm*'s killer spheres on tour shirts, Ice-T has always been an ambassador for the horror genre. This song wasn't the only time he sampled Black Sabbath, either. He used them again, very effectively, on "Midnight".

BEV: I'm far more familiar with Ice-T as Detective Fin Tutuola on *Law & Order: SVU* than I am with him as a musician, to be honest. This track will certainly set the mood, with the sound of thunder and rain followed by an emergency alert list of rules that sounds like it's straight out of *1984* or *A Clockwork Orange*. Anyone who listens to this song MAY BE SHOT.

Track 2: Everything's Ruined by Faith No More (album: *Angel Dust*)

BRIAN: I had a definite theme in mind for my playlist. You'll probably pick up on it very quickly. I chose this track—one of my favorite songs by one of my favorite bands—because it was upbeat and heavy and mixed nicely with Ice-T's introduction, and yet it promises with each chorus that everything is indeed ruined, and it's only going to get worse from here on out.

BEV: Many (many) years ago, my coworker, his wife and I went to see a Billy Idol concert in Houston. This was at the Summit, a building that is now home to one of Joel Osteen's megachurches. Faith No More was the opening act. The guitar player had long, long hair that he flung around while he played, casting off sweat in all directions. They didn't do a terribly good job of cleaning up the stage afterward, because Billy Idol's guitar player slipped in the puddle and fell when they took the stage. I didn't care for this song much on first listen, but it grew on me after a while. Reminded me of something off a freebie CD we got at a World Horror Convention a while back: *The Vampire Ball*.

Track 3: One Step Up by Bruce Springsteen (album: *Tunnel of Love*)

BRIAN: Author John Skipp once provided me with a promotional blurb that said, "If Brian Keene's books were music, they would occupy a well-earned space between Bruce Springsteen, Neil Young, and Eminem." That remains the nicest thing anyone has ever said about me. Springsteen's

DISSONANT HARMONIES

music has been a constant in my life since middle-school. He's gotten me through trials and tribulations and triumphs and high point and low points. And I love that his music changes as I change.

BEV: A long time ago, when the earth was green, there were these things called record clubs, of which Columbia House was the most famous. You paid a penny to sign up and got a dozen or so records, committing to purchase a certain number of records over the course of the next year. Each month, there was a default selection; if you didn't cancel it on time, it was shipped to you automatically, and sending it back wasn't easy. That's how I ended up with Springsteen's *Nebraska* album. I hated that record. I like maybe a third of Springsteen's more popular songs. This one is quite good—and a jarring change from the previous track on this playlist!

Track 4: Not Dark Yet by Bob Dylan (album: *Time Out of Mind*)

BRIAN: Bob Dylan has always been hit and miss with me, but this song…this song kicks me in my soul. Easily my favorite by him, and it fits the theme quite nicely.

BEV: My music horizons exploded during my first year at university. After growing up in a village, where the nearest town didn't have a record store, my exposure to music was limited to the stuff that was available on the local A.M. radio station. All definitely Top 40 stuff. Suddenly I discovered a whole new world of music, some of it incredible. And then there was *Slow Train Coming*, the new Dylan album that year. I still like to make fun of "Gotta Serve Somebody," which I can sing with a nasally twang. It took me a while to recover from that. My favorite Dylan work was the collaboration he did with the Traveling Wilburys. This song is a good follow-up to the Springsteen, though. Very listenable.

Track 5: Outlaw Shit by Waylon Jennings (album: *Waylon Forever*)

BRIAN: My parents were big fans of country music, and it was always on in our house. Even as a kid, the Outlaw stuff (typified by Waylon, Johnny Cash, Willie Nelson, etc) was my favorite country sub-genre (much to my father's delight and my mother's chagrin). They were very much the Splatterpunks of country music, and were treated the same as Joe R. Lansdale, David J. Schow and Skipp and Spector were early on. Waylon's original version of this song is a toe-tapping barn boogie that serves as a response to their then-critics, but decades later, he recorded this slower, more maudlin remake. The lyrics are the same, but the song takes on an all new mournful and darker meaning.

BEV: This is much more like the music I heard growing up. We were a bastion of country music, especially on daytime radio, although this song, with its expletive title, would never have made the cut in a million years. Hell, even Spotify asterisked out the title in Brian's playlist. I have a fondness for these old outlaws—Cash, Kristofferson, Nelson and their ilk. This is a melancholy song about being branded something by the media (or the law) by someone who is fed up with being labeled.

Track 6: I See a Darkness by Johnny Cash (album: *American III: Solitary Man*)

BRIAN: I liked this song years before everyone else heard it on AMC's *The Walking Dead*. It dovetails perfectly with the preceding track.

BEV: Of all the performers on this list, Cash is probably the only one that my parents would have *listened* to! I remember when he played the celebrity murderer on an episode of *Columbo*, and I thought that was pretty cool.

Track 7: When It's Cold I'd Like to Die by Moby (album: *Everything is Wrong*)

BRIAN: I can't say that I'm a Moby fan. All I know of his music is "Extreme Ways" (from the Jason Bourne movie franchise) and this song, which closes my favorite single episode of *The Sopranos*, in which the main character hovers between life and death in a coma or an alternate universe (you decide). The song—and that scene—give me chills every time.

BEV: I'm not sure I've heard a Moby song before this. I'm starting to detect a theme. Darkness, loneliness, ruination, the end of times. Oddly enough, though I listened to this music over and over again while I wrote *The Dead of Winter* (a title that sounds bleak, too), I think my novella is fairly light and cheery. Go figure.

DISSONANT HARMONIES

Track 8: Praying for Time by George Michael (album: *Listen without Prejudice Vol. 1*)

BRIAN: There was a time, years before his death, when people only remembered George Michael for the bubblegum dance pop of the Wham era. They would argue with me that he never recorded anything of lasting consequence. When they did this, I would play this track and they'd then shut the fuck up.

BEV: Does anyone these days remember Wham!? The "group" from which Michael emerged. Wow, I'm dating myself. This song has the big sound of the eighties, though it's technically a nineties song. It's a good preamble to what comes next. I don't think Michael and Mercury ever did a duet, did they? That would have been great.

Track 9: The Show Must Go On by Queen (album: *Innuendo*)

BRIAN: I've come to terms with the loss of Tom Petty, David Bowie, Prince, Neil Peart, and Motörhead's Lemmy...but man, I still miss Freddie Mercury. Greatest vocalist of all time.

BEV: Bullseye! This is the one song from the playlist that you'd find in my music library—and my library consists of thousands and thousands of tracks. This song is gut-wrenching, especially when you watch the video and realize that Freddie Mercury's health was in such a bad state when they were recording it, but he still gave it his all. He's one of the greats—what a voice. I remember when they came out at Live Aid and blew the roof off the place. People generally thought of them as a studio band because their songs were so hard to perform live, but they showed everyone that day.

Track 10: Nutshell by Alice in Chains (album: *Unplugged*)

BRIAN: I've done karaoke exactly six times in my life. Four of those times, it was to this song. One of the truest odes to fame and addiction and the glare of the public eye that I've ever heard. In some ways, it's a bookend to Pink Floyd's "Have a Cigar" (and by the way, which one's Pink?).

BEV: Another act that I couldn't have named a song by to save my life. I thought maybe I was getting a mellowed-out version since Spotify queued up the Unplugged album version, so I tracked down the original album version. It's not all that different. I guess I expected AiC to be more metal, but that's just my uninformed preconception. In case an overall theme hadn't hit me yet, here we have a song about misprinted lies, facing it all alone, and a loss of privacy. I'd feel better dead, the dude says. (Which one's Alice?)

Track 11: Man That You Fear by Marilyn Manson (album: *Antichrist Superstar*)

BRIAN: Back in 2009, I had what used to be called "a nervous breakdown". I prefer the term "I lost my shit". Two friends found me in my underwear, comatose, with this song playing on endless repeat over the stereo. They thought I was dead. I did, too. I still love the track, but these days, it reminds me of where I've been and where I am now.

BEV: I was intrigued to hear that Manson would be appearing on *Sons of Anarchy*. Musicians sometimes make the crossover to acting, but often they don't. I thought he did a decent job, especially in such a vile role. This feels like a direct sequel to the Ice-T song, for some reason. It has a good beat, but I'm not sure I could dance to it. So, just in case there were any doubts, everything is turning to shit and you can kill yourself now!

Track 12: Beside You in Time by Nine Inch Nails (album: *With Teeth*)

BRIAN: Much like Alice in Chains' "Nutshell", this entire album deals with fame and the public eye. It's my favorite by Nine Inch Nails, and is usually in heavy rotation, no matter what I'm writing.

BEV: I always felt like I should like Nine Inch Nails better than I do. There was an album they gave away a few years ago, *Ghosts*, that I downloaded and listened to a couple of times, but I couldn't get into it. I'm still not sure, after many, many listens, whether I like this song or not. It's mesmerizing, I'll give it that. Gets a little tedious after a while, though. While I normally like electronica, which is what this reminds me of, though it isn't really, it gets on my nerves, to be honest—and then it doesn't because the transition at the end does something quite interesting.

DISSONANT HARMONIES

Track 13: Right Where it Belongs by Nine Inch Nails (album: *With Teeth*)

BRIAN: See my comments above. The only thing I'd add is listen to what Trent Reznor does here with sound engineering when you hear the sounds of the crowd applauding. It's an audible haunted house novel.

BEV: This will never be my favorite band, but this song is easier to listen to than the previous. It has the feel of a song where one person is playing all the instruments, though. Not that that's a bad thing.

Track 14: Redford by Sufjan Stevens (album: *Michigan*)

BRIAN: Another one I discovered via *The Sopranos*, and simultaneously a respite from what Bev has been exposed to so far, and a moody segue into what comes next, as the mixtape builds to its conclusion.

BEV: I was really surprised to see Sufjan Stevens on this playlist, because I only encountered him through listening to CBC radio. This is a simple piano track with a simple melody that provides a welcome respite from the dire lyrics on the list so far. It's almost inspirational!

Track 15: All of This Could Have Been Yours by Hierophant (album: *Black Ribbons*)

BRIAN: This song got me through my second divorce. The whole album is great, and Shooter was kind enough to let me use the lyrics from another track as an epigraph in one of my novels, but this song right here? This is perfection.

BEV: Okay, I lied. This is the other track that I have in my music library. How could I not, given that the album has Stephen King doing a bit between songs? And a lyric that is borrowed from a King short story: All that you love will be carried away. I have to confess that my tastes run more toward piano/keyboard performers than guitarists, so this one is right up my alley. I like this song a lot.

Track 16: King for a Day by Faith No More (album: *King for a Day, Fool for a Lifetime*)

BEV VINCENT & BRIAN KEENE

BRIAN: Well, after the utter emotional and sonic pathos of the previous song, I needed to give Bev something uplifting and jaunty. But I also needed to keep with the overall theme. So, I went back to Faith No More, because nobody is better at juggling both. "Don't let me die with that silly look in my eyes…"

BEV: This is one of my favorite songs on the list. It's bouncy and upbeat, with this great guitar rhythm and a funny, gravelly vocal rendition. It gets a little scream-o in places, but it's still a fun song.

So, there you have it. Those were our mix tapes and what each of us listened to as we wrote our novellas.

Here are the results.

—Bev Vincent and Brian Keene

The Dead of Winter

Bev Vincent

For Mary Anne and Virginia

1

JOEY WAS SUPPOSED to pick Frank up from T.F. Green at 6:30, but he was still coming down from the hit of acid he'd taken after lunch and time had gotten away from him. Under normal conditions, it took forty-five minutes to get to the Providence airport from Bayport, but conditions were far from ideal. Not only was Joey seeing surreal colors and having bizarre visions, it had been snowing since dawn and Joey hadn't put the winter tires on his Civic yet. In fact, he had no idea where they were. Under the garage, maybe, or in the basement. Joey had a habit of losing track of stuff, even big things like steel-belted radials.

Eric was still relatively straight—he'd only been smoking pot and polishing off a case of beer—so Joey asked him to drive. Joey sat in the back seat so he didn't have to watch the snowflakes streaming toward the windshield like something out of a science fiction movie. Even seeing them carom off the side window was freaking him out.

He hoped his brother's flight would be late, what with the weather and all. But no, as luck would have it, Frank's plane landed a few minutes early. He called Joey while the aircraft was taxiing to the gate. Joey assured him they'd be there by the time Frank picked up his bags. They hadn't yet exited onto 195, so that was a lie, but Joey dealt those like cards at a poker game.

By the time they reached the airport exit, it was well after seven o'clock. Traffic *had* been bad, and they'd encountered a couple of wrecks that slowed them down, but still. Joey texted his brother to meet them outside the arrivals area, saying they'd be there in a few minutes. Texting was easier than talking, especially where his brother was concerned. There'd be enough time for talk on the long drive back to Bayport.

Eric, who had done a primo job of driving in Joey's opinion, pulled into an empty spot in front of the United exit and popped the back hatch. Joey wiped condensation off the side window and looked for Frank. "There he is," he said. "Honk the horn or flash the lights or something." Eric seemed flustered by these instructions, so Joey pushed the passenger seat up, leaned forward and rolled down the window. He stuck his hand out and waved, trying to catch Frank's attention. A gust of cold air overwhelmed the aging car's heater. Joey pulled his jacket tight and waved again. "Over here, asshole," he said through clenched teeth.

Frank suddenly looked in their direction, as if he'd intuited the words. He dragged his rolling suitcase toward the car. "Back's open," Joey called out before cranking up the window. He supposed he could have gotten out and greeted his brother properly, but it was freaking cold out there, and the flakes were still zooming at him a little too fast for comfort.

The car shook when Frank slammed the hatch, and another cold gust swept through the interior when he opened the passenger door and got in. Joey was about to say something, make a crack about how hot it must be back in Houston, but Frank beat him to the punch. Without a glance into the back seat, he peered at Eric, who was fiddling with the wipers. "You're in no shape to drive," he said. Always had to be a cop, Joey thought. Even now.

"Naw, man, I'm good," Eric said.

"No way. I can smell it from here. I'll drive."

Another blast of Arctic air as he got out. Eric glanced over his shoulder and shrugged, but he didn't argue when Frank opened his door and waited for him to vacate the driver's seat.

"When's the last time you drove in snow?" Joey asked.

Frank didn't answer. He put the car into gear and pulled away from the curb.

"You might want to take it easy," Joey said after the car fishtailed at a stoplight.

"And why's that?"

"No winter tires," Joey said.

"Figures," Frank said, though his voice was so low Joey almost didn't hear him.

THE DEAD OF WINTER

The trio remained silent for the first several miles while Frank got a feel for the car and road conditions. Joey was tempted to ask his older brother if he still knew the way home, but for once he kept his mouth shut.

I-95 was in rough condition, and traffic was heavy. A few minutes after Frank took the exit onto 195 headed toward Massachusetts, he interrupted the silence. "No news, I assume?"

Joey had been tranced out, staring at streetlights floating past and the snow swirling around them. "Huh?"

"About Donna. Anything new?"

"No, man. Nothing." He glanced at Eric in the front seat, dozing against the passenger window. "Still gone. Just like the others."

The car slipped to the left. Frank corrected but couldn't hide his surprise. "Others?"

Joey savored the moment. "Donna was the fifth. Didn't you know?"

Frank kept his eyes on the road. "All women?"

"No. She was the only one. Well, Mrs. McCarthy, but she's like almost fifty."

"Let me get this straight," Frank said. "Five people are missing? In Bayport?"

Joey nodded. "Yeah, that's right."

"Why am I just hearing about this now?"

"I'll bet people go missing in Houston all the time. Killed, too, probably."

"But five people in a town of 3000? Since when?"

"It's gotten smaller since you left," Joey said. He doubted Frank could see his smirk in the rearview mirror in the dark.

"Since when?" Frank repeated.

Joey thought about it. "Eddie went a year ago in January. Everyone thought he just left. Went to Providence or someplace to get work. But his mom hasn't heard from him since. I hear he hasn't touched his bank account, either."

"Eddie? Eddie who?"

"How many Eddies we know?" Joey asked. "Or did you forget about everyone once you went to the big city?"

"Eddie Jamieson."

"Uh-huh."

"Donna, Mrs. McCarthy—you mean Joker's mom?"

"Uh-huh."

"Who else?"

"Harvey Andrews. Mr. Thompson."

"The math teacher?"

"Yep. School's out for that motherfucker." Joey giggled. The acid had mostly worn off and he was left with this expansive, refreshing sensation like his mind had been rebooted. Taken out of his skull, rinsed off and replaced. He felt pretty chill, actually, despite having to talk to his asshole brother. The guy who hadn't come home the whole time their dad was sick, not until it was too late, at least, but who dropped everything the second he heard about his former high school girlfriend, who he probably hadn't talked to in, what, ten years at least?

The car was quiet again, except for Eric's snores. The snow was still falling heavily, but Frank didn't seem to be having any problem with the road. The car skidded a bit on the ramp when he exited to Route 24, but he recovered without making the situation worse. He'd probably learned all sorts of fancy car tricks in the police academy, Joey thought. "No trouble getting time off?" he asked. He didn't mean it as a dig, except he kinda did.

Frank didn't answer right away. "Not really," he said about a mile farther down the road, by which time Joey had almost forgotten the question.

The only place Frank ran into trouble was when he reached the house. Joey hadn't cleaned out the driveway for a while—he was too busy getting high and playing *Final Fantasy XIV*—so today's storm made it nearly impassable. They couldn't leave the car on the street, though. At some point Hector would get his lazy ass out of bed and behind the wheel of the snowplow, and woe to any vehicle that stood in his way.

Joey said, "We got this." He roused Eric and the two of them scooped a path down the middle of the driveway while Frank idled at the curb. After a few minutes, Joey was exhausted and overheating, so he waved his brother in. The car got stuck halfway to the garage. Frank spun the tires for a few seconds, then tried rocking the car back and forth, but it wouldn't budge. Joey and Eric made a half-hearted stab at pushing, but Joey didn't really care, so long as the car was off the street. They'd worry about it tomorrow. Or the day after. Maybe he'd look for the snow tires, too. They had to be somewhere, didn't they? "That's good," Joey said, slapping the roof over Frank's head as if that had been the plan all along.

Eric gave Joey a mock salute and staggered off into the snowy night. "Later, dude," he said. He only lived a couple of blocks away, so Joey wasn't overly concerned about him.

THE DEAD OF WINTER

Joey and Frank slogged through the drifts, knee-deep in places, to the side porch door. It was warmer inside the house, though not by much. Furnace oil was expensive and Joey hadn't been getting much work lately. Things were always slow during the winter, but to be honest he hadn't been looking all that hard. As long as he had enough cash for pizza, beer and grass, he was fine. The acid had been a treat, something to take the edge off before Frank arrived. He had a feeling he'd need it.

Frank sniffed the air and looked around the kitchen. The sink was filled with a heap of dirty dishes, and empty pizza boxes were stacked haphazardly on the countertop, surrounded by battalions of beer bottles. Joey waited for the snide comment that was sure to come, but Frank kept his opinions to himself.

Frank hadn't been home since their father's funeral, three years ago. It had been winter then, too. Both of their parents had gone in the wintertime, which meant internment in the vault until spring, when the ground thawed. Frank hadn't returned for the committal service so it had just been Joey and a few people from around town who always turned out for these things. Joey didn't blame him, not for that. He'd wished at the time he could have been somewhere—anywhere—else, too. He'd been hung over and bleary-eyed, and the sound of the minister's voice droning on about ashes and dust had made his head hurt like a motherfucker.

He did blame Frank for not being there before, though, when he needed help with the old man, who'd gotten cantankerous and uncooperative as the dementia worsened. But, no, Frank was working his way up in the world, his eyes on the gold badge, and he couldn't afford to take time off. In retrospect, Joey supposed his brother hadn't taken time off for anything, including his wife—ex-wife, that is—who had sought companionship elsewhere during the lonely hours while her husband pulled OT and worked like a grunt to better his position.

At least that was how Joey liked to imagine things going down. He'd never met the former Mrs. Shaw. Melissa, her name was. He'd been invited to the wedding but couldn't afford the trip to Houston. That was his excuse, anyway. The truth was, he might have swung it, but he resented the hell out of his brother for finding a way to escape Bayport, and he couldn't stand the thought of seeing him in his happy new life in the big city. Since the marriage didn't take, he figured he'd done himself a favor, not wasting money on the airfare. Or a gift, come to think of it.

Frank was still standing just inside the door, as if awaiting an invitation to come in. It was as much his place as Joey's, though. They'd each received an equal share in the will, but it had been up to Joey to handle all the red tape to finalize the estate. The old man had left behind a small legacy—bigger than Joey might have guessed, once the dust settled—and it had delighted Joey in no small measure to send his brother the check for his share. He'd been absolutely scrupulous about the bookkeeping in case Frank accused him of cheating, but the issue never came up and Joey got to live in the house so long as he paid the taxes and utilities. That was saving him a bundle on rent.

Frank unzipped his coat—the same one he'd worn the last time he was here, Joey observed. Probably not much call for winter gear in Texas. He didn't take it off, though, which Joey took as a hint. He twisted the dial on the thermostat. "It'll take a while to warm up," he said. "I was out most of the day."

Another lie.

Frank nodded. "I could use a beer. Do you have any?" Joey glanced at the empties lined up on the countertop and wondered if Frank was making fun of him. He chose to ignore the jab, if it was one, and got a Narragansett from the fridge. He didn't take one for himself. As long as Frank was here, he planned to play it cool. Keep his head straight.

As his brother moved across the kitchen, Joey scrutinized him for changes since the last time he'd seen him, but Frank looked much the same as always. Maybe a hint of gray woven into his jet-black hair, but no paunch from too many doughnuts on the job.

Frank took a seat at the kitchen table, around which the family of four once spent some of their best hours. There was almost always a jigsaw puzzle going back then, covered by a thin sheet of Plexiglas during meal times, and they played cards and board games there, too. They'd always eaten together when their schedules allowed, something that became harder as the boys got older and became involved in athletics (Frank) and theater (Joey). Good times, Joey thought.

"So," Frank said after his first swig of beer. "Tell me about the disappearances."

2

"Do you want something to eat?" Joey looked around the kitchen. "I think I'm all out of fatted calves to kill, though." The truth was, he didn't have a clue what was on hand. Canned beans, maybe, unless he'd scarfed the last of those down when he had the munchies.

"I'm fine," Frank said. "I had plenty of time at the airport, so I grabbed a burger."

Again, it felt like a dig, but just about everything that came out of Frank's mouth did. It had always been that way between them.

Joey nodded, filled a glass with water from the tap and sat across from his brother. He took a sip and tried to figure out how to begin.

"It's different, living here as a grown-up, you know? When we were kids, it was the best place in the world. Small. Secluded. Safe. Everybody knew everyone. But once you're out of school, once you grow up, things change. It's not small—it's stifling. It's not secluded—it's fucking miles from anywhere. You have to drive thirty miles to take a leak. And as for safer? Well, you wouldn't know, would you, because you caught the first freight train you could out of here. Moved halfway across the continent and never looked back."

Joey paused for a breath and another sip of water. Frank tipped his head to acknowledge the accusation. This was old territory, well trodden. Nothing to be gained by going over it again. But he was still trying to find his way into the story.

"People were sure you'd go somewhere on a football scholarship. You and Donna forever, like. But instead you took off. Someday you'll have to tell me how you wound up in Houston, of all places." He shrugged. "Left me here all alone. Oh, sure, I had Mom and Dad at first, but once you were gone, I didn't know what to do with myself. No one was going to give me a scholarship and I didn't see any point in getting a degree in English, which was about the only thing I was good at. So I stayed and plugged away at one thing or another after graduation and, before you know it, ten years passed, and what do I have to show for it? What do any of us who live in this godforsaken place?"

Another sigh. Another sip of water. Frank didn't say a word, just took a hit from his beer.

"So, anyway, when people disappear in the middle of the night, no forwarding address...when they just leave everything behind and get the fuck out of Dodge, who can blame them? Good on ya, mate." He raised his water glass in a mock toast.

"For example, when people realized Eddie wasn't around anymore, wasn't hanging out at Sal's, wasn't squealing his tires down Main Street, wasn't smacking some girl around and ending up in the drunk tank, everyone figured he'd had enough and hightailed it. Except his truck was still here, and all his shit was at his apartment and his bank account wasn't touched—not that there was much in it to touch. His mama kept asking around and eventually someone called the police, but nothing. No crime scene, no body, no suspects. Nothing. Everyone was happy to go on believing he took a powder and someday he'd send his mama a postcard from Florida or California or Fiji. Good riddance."

"And this was January, last year?" Frank asked.

"Fucking harsh winter that was. This one's sizing up to be the same. Yeah, the last time anyone remembered seeing him for sure was the week after New Year's. Then the math teacher didn't show up at school one morning. You remember Thompson. He was older than God when we had him, but he never missed a day."

"When was this?"

"February. Groundhog Day. I remember, because people were joking he must have seen his shadow and gone back home for six weeks. The school checked on him the next day, when he didn't show up again and didn't answer his phone."

"No family?"

Joey shook his head. "Outlived them all, I guess."

"What did they find at his place?"

"Car in the garage, mail in the box, food in the fridge, cat on the prowl. No signs of a disturbance."

"And no body."

"Right. That, too. The popular theory was that he got Alzheimer's or something and wandered off during a snowstorm."

"Alzheimer's? Overnight?"

"Or a stroke." Joey shrugged. "Want another beer?"

Frank shook his head, then paused. "Why not? It's been a long day."

"I didn't ask how your flight was," Joey said.

"I noticed. What were you on? Must've been some strong shit for you to let Eric drive, half in the bag like he was."

Joey shrugged again and went to the fridge to fetch another beer for his brother, resisting the temptation to get one for

THE DEAD OF WINTER

himself. Instead he refilled his water glass at the tap before returning to the table. Digging up all this old history was a drag, but he wasn't going to let anything interfere with his post-trip euphoria.

"Who's next?" Frank asked.

"Joker's mom. Everyone figured she got fed up with her husband's shit and took off, maybe with some other guy, but she didn't take her car or anything, either."

"And this was in...?"

"Last March. Yeah, I'm pretty sure. We had that big storm on St. Patrick's Day."

"A year ago."

"Yep. Joker was pretty messed up about it. He got into a brawl with his dad and spent a few days in jail."

"He has no idea where she went?"

"He's not saying, but I think he thinks his old man killed her and disposed of the body."

"And no one was worried when three people disappeared over the course of a couple of months?"

"It was winter. You know what that's like—or maybe you don't remember. People don't get out, so there's not as much gossip. I suppose everyone was waiting for the snow to melt and turn up a body or two. But, like I said, that was a brutal winter and by the time the snow was gone, everybody had pretty much forgotten about them."

Frank shook his head. He was playing with the label on his beer bottle, Joey noticed. An old habit. By the time he was finished with the beer, he'd have both the front and back labels peeled off. Funny how some things never change, he mused.

"So, after that, things were quiet for a while?"

"Shit, bro. Things are *always* quiet around here. Disappearing math teachers and housewives, that hardly caused a blip on the radar. People are like, I wonder whatever happened to so-and-so, and then it's back to the daily grind. Folks have too much on their own plates without worrying about anyone else, nosy as they might seem."

Frank finished peeling the front label off his beer bottle and laid it on top of the one from the first bottle. "So, all summer long, nothing."

"No one vanished, if that's what you mean. People went about their business. One or two of them died." He saw the curiosity on Frank's face. "Natural causes, if you call getting crushed by your car while you're working under it 'natural.'"

Around here, maybe it is." He took a sip of water. "Henry Murchie. I don't think you know him. He's from away. Took over Sheldon's garage after Sheldon had to sell."

"When did it start again?" Frank's fingernails tapped on the bottle as he started on the back label.

"If by 'it' you mean people vanishing, a couple of months ago."

"January."

"Yeah. Just after the new year."

"Hm."

"What?"

"Nothing. It's just that I'm starting to see a pattern."

"Oh, sure. Like those smart cops on TV. A pattern."

Frank held up his hand and raised his thumb and first two fingers in sequence. "Last year January, February, March." He closed his hand and repeated the process. "This year, January, February." He left his middle finger half bent this time. Joey understood what he was getting at but wouldn't give him the satisfaction of acknowledging it.

"So, yeah, Harvey Andrews in January."

"What's the story there?"

"He used to teach at the University.

"Roger Williams."

"No, Yale, you doofus. Of course RWU. Retired a year or so ago. Kept pretty much to himself. I think he was writing something. The secret history of the Rhode Island Red or the Necronomicon or some shit. I was never inside his place, but people said it was like a library, only neater."

"Who noticed he was gone?"

"He had a woman who cooked his meals. Theresa Whitaker—remember her? Easy Theresee? You must have had a piece of that. Everyone did."

Frank didn't respond.

"She said he would've starved to death if someone didn't cook for him. She went in twice a day, morning and suppertime. Maybe she was banging him, too. Who knows? Anyway, he was there when she went in that morning but gone when she stopped off after work. She's at the nail salon on Milton Street. She thought it was odd, but she left his dinner in the oven, keeping it warm but not so it would burn. It was still there the next morning, dried all to hell. She kept checking back, but nada."

"Did he have family?"

"A daughter in Pensacola and a son in Wyoming. They'd last spoken with him on New Year's Eve."
"And nothing since. No word."
"Nada."
"And then there was Donna."
Joey nodded. "You know all about that. Probably more than me."
"Tell me anyway. Tell me what you know."

3

"When did you last see her?" Joey asked.
"We talked a little after Dad's funeral."
"Did you meet her husband?"
Frank shook his head.
"Just as well. You probably would have kicked his ass."
"That bad?"
"Pure-g asshole from top to bottom."
"She seemed, I dunno, anxious that day."
"It was a funeral, after all. No one was at their best." Joey took a drink to wet his lips. "But she was probably afraid he'd find out she was talking to you."
"He beat her?"
"Only on weekends," Joey said. "And weekdays."
Frank got up from the table and stared out the kitchen window into the darkness. "Still snowing," he said. "How'd she get away from him?"
"He got into it with a guy at a convenience store. Something to do with lottery tickets, I gather. He beat the dude so bad he was in the hospital for two weeks. The guy pressed charges and Mr. Cro-Magnon went away for a while. Donna took the opportunity to move her stuff out."
"When was this?"
"Last fall. September, or thereabouts."
"When did her husband get out of jail?"
"A few months later. Christmas. She was pretty worried about it."
"You seem to know a lot about her situation."
Joey thought about the beer left in the fridge, but he was determined to stick to his resolve. "Small town," he said. He took a breath. "I helped her move," he said after a lengthy pause. "We were good friends, a while back."

Frank raised an eyebrow. "How long ago?"

"Coupla years after you blew town. We ran into each other at Sal's, had a few drinks. You know. Talked. It happens."

"But it didn't last."

Joey shrugged. "Never does."

"But when she needed help..."

"I was happy to lend a hand. We ran into each other all the time. We stayed friendly, but it was tough after she married that jerk."

"Why did she?"

"Got pregnant. She lost the kid, but by then the damage was done."

"So, the husband—what's his name?"

"Luke. Luke Stevens."

"Could he have done something to her?"

"Oh yeah. It's what everyone in town is thinking. He says he has an alibi, was with some other chick, but he'd be high on my list of suspects."

"Except..."

"Except."

"There's a pattern."

"So you said."

"Five people missing. Three men, two women. All of them...older."

"Not exactly ancient."

"But not the typical targets of a serial killer."

"In case you haven't noticed—and how could you?—that demographic is pretty much the norm around here. We have a conspicuous population gap in the 20 to 35 range."

"You stayed."

"Oh yeah. I guess I did. Thanks for pointing that out."

Frank finished peeling the back label from his beer and smoothed it on the tabletop.

"So, what now? Why are you here?"

Frank shook his head. "Old business, I guess. Donna and I didn't part on the best of terms, and when I saw her..."

"...at Dad's funeral..."

Frank nodded. "I didn't exactly improve matters. Looking back on it now—and based on what you're telling me—maybe she was looking for my help, and I more or less blew her off."

"You think she saw you as her knight in shining armor?"

Frank didn't respond.

Joey came at it from a different angle. "You think the local police aren't doing their job."

THE DEAD OF WINTER

Frank's eyes grew dark. "If they haven't looked for a connection among these cases—if they aren't worried about five people simply vanishing—I don't think they know what their job is."

"And you're here to set them straight."

"I'm here to do what I can."

"How did you find out about Donna? It's not like you're staying in close touch with anyone here."

Frank's mouth turned into a straight line, as if he were about to take issue with his brother's observation. Then he exhaled loudly. "Her mother asked me to help."

"Donna's mother called you in Texas?"

"She emailed me but, yes, she reached out."

"After all this time."

Frank shrugged. "What can I say? She liked me."

"Everyone liked you," Joey said. He glanced at the wall clock. All this talk had exhausted him and his voice was getting hoarse. He'd said more in the last hour than he normally did in a week. "I'm gonna crash," he said. "Your old room is ready." Joey usually bunked out on the living room couch, but he didn't want his brother to know that.

"Busy day tomorrow?"

"Same number of hours as all the rest," Joey said before mounting the stairs and collapsing onto his bed.

4

"It's still coming down out there," Frank said the next morning when Joey stumbled downstairs. It was 8:30 and Joey was wrung out from his acid trip the day before, and the long, mostly one-sided conversation with his brother.

"Winter sucks," he said. "You made coffee?"

"Yep," Frank said. "The milk's gone off, but you like yours black, if I remember."

Joey pulled a cup from the sink, wincing when the dishes clattered, rinsed it out and poured a full cup. It smelled wonderful. "What's the forecast?" he asked.

Frank pulled out his phone and played with the settings. "Snow...snow...and more snow." He pocketed the device. "I'd forgotten how much you have to pay attention to the weather around here. Unless there's a storm in the Gulf of Mexico, you can pretty much predict what any given day will be like in Houston."

Joey sipped his coffee. He could feel the caffeine rushing through his veins. He was rarely organized enough to make it for himself in the morning. In fact, he was surprised there was any in the house. And when had he last bought milk?

"What's your plan for today?" he asked.

"Thought I'd check in with the police chief. Let him know I'm here, poking around."

"Her," Joey said.

"Huh?"

"Lauren Morton is the chief of police," he said.

"Okay."

Joey looked out the window. There was at least a foot of new snow in the yard. "Until I get the winter tires on my car, I don't think it's going anywhere."

"Guess I'll walk, then. Want to come with? Make introductions? I assume you're on a first name basis with most of the cops around here."

"Ha, ha," Joey said. "Ho, ho."

"Come on. We can get something to eat on the way."

Visiting the police station wasn't high on Joey's list of favorite things to do, but he was curious to see how the meeting would go. How Chief Morton would react to the news that the big Texas cop was sticking his nose into one of her cases. He wouldn't mind seeing Frank get his ass handed to him. Besides, he was hungry and it sounded like his brother might be buying.

He almost changed his mind when he opened the door to a wall of snow. Though he had on his tall boots and a parka, the wind quickly chilled him to the bone. He wrapped a scarf around his mouth and nose, pulled on fleece-lined gloves and forced his way through the drifts on the steps. His only consolation was the fact that his brother was probably less thrilled about going out in this weather than he was. Frank had been in Texas long enough for his blood to have thinned. He wouldn't be used to cold like this anymore.

The streets hadn't been plowed yet, so the only vehicles moving were four-wheel drives and trucks, and even they were proceeding at a crawl. The sidewalks were no treat, either. Joey was almost ready to turn around and go home when they discovered the coffee shop at the corner of Juniper and Cherry wasn't open; however, the grocery store a block away on Willow Avenue was, so they got breakfast in the deli department. Bacon, eggs and hash browns for Joey, and a bagel with lox and cream cheese for Frank. The coffee was

THE DEAD OF WINTER

fresh and strong. At first, they were the only customers in the deli, but others slowly drifted in while they ate. No one gave Joey a second glance, though a couple of people looked at Frank like they thought they might recognize him.

The police station was quiet, too. The receptionist was hanging up her winter coat and changing her boots for shoes when they arrived. She glanced at Joey and wrinkled her nose. He and Patty had history, but it had been a while since they'd been out.

"Who's your friend?" Patty asked with obvious interest.

"Detective Frank Shaw," Frank said, offering her his hand. "From Houston, here to see Chief Morton."

Patty looked from Joey to Frank and back to Joey. "Your brother?"

"Detective?" Joey asked. "When did that happen?"

"A year or so ago."

"You never said."

Frank shrugged. "We don't talk all that much. As you said." He returned his attention to Patty. "I'm sorry, Miss…"

"Gilroy. Patty Gilroy."

"I'm sorry, Miss Gilroy. Is the Chief in?"

"Don't suppose you have an appointment," she said, leafing through the day planner on her desk.

"Afraid not."

"The reason for your visit?"

"A courtesy call, to let the chief know Donna Conrad's mother asked me if I would look into her disappearance."

Patty pursed her lips, a look that was familiar to Joey. "Let me check."

After she disappeared into the chief's office, Joey turned to his brother. "The gold badge. Woo-eee. Guess it all paid off."

"What?"

"All that work. All those long hours."

Frank frowned. Joey knew he was probably waiting for a snarky comment, so he just left him hanging. He could have congratulated him, he supposed. It was sort of a big deal. But it was apparently old news, so he said nothing.

"The chief will see you now," Patty said when she emerged a few minutes later.

"I'll wait out here," Joey said.

Frank shook his head, giving him the big brother look that said he'd kick Joey's ass if he didn't go along. Joey hadn't seen that look in many years, but he remembered it well and had no doubt Frank could still whip him if he decided to. Joey might get in a few good licks—he'd once dislocated his brother's shoulder during one of their otherwise one-sided wrestling matches—but in the end he'd go down for the count. He got up and followed Frank into the chief's office.

As soon as he saw the uncomfortable glance between his brother and Bayport's chief of police, Joey remembered that there was history there, too. Once upon a time, Frank had been the leading pass receiver for the Bayport Buccaneers and Lauren had been a cheerleader. It would have been more of a cliché only if Frank had been the quarterback, but his arm hadn't been up to that. Back then, she had been Lauren Franklin, which was probably why Frank hadn't made the connection until now. This little reunion could be more entertaining than Joey had anticipated.

"As I live and breathe," Chief Morton said. "Look what the cat dragged all the way from—where was it? Austin? Phoenix?"

"Houston," Frank said.

"Knew it was someplace hot." She didn't so much as look at Joey. All her attention was on Frank, which gave Joey plenty of time to size her up. She was a few years older than he was—Frank's age—and Joey had been gaga over her when he was a teenager. She'd gone away after high school, gotten married, studied criminal law, gotten divorced and returned to Bayport last summer to take over the department after Chief Collins died of a heart attack while sitting at his desk. This very desk, in fact. There was a man who'd enjoyed his doughnuts.

Joey had always been peripherally aware of Morton lurking in the background the few times he'd stopped by the station to pick Patty up, but she intimidated him. Redheads had a tendency to do that, plus there was the fact that she was a cop. And tall, to boot—nearly as tall as he was. Under her carefully shaped eyebrows, she had crystalline green eyes that took in everything, as if you couldn't keep any secrets from her, which was probably useful in her job. She'd maintained her cheerleader's toned body, too, he gathered, based on the way her uniform looked on her. He could still picture her shaking her pom-poms on the sidelines, a memory that had fueled many teenaged fantasies. Now she was packing .44s. He put a hand over his mouth to shield a grin.

"Presenting yourself as a peace officer from a foreign jurisdiction, I gather," Morton said. She seemed to be enjoying herself. "I suppose I should ask to see some ID. To be all formal and everything."

THE DEAD OF WINTER

Frank reached inside his coat, but Morton put out her palms and laughed. "I'm kidding, Frank. Boy, you never did have much of a sense of humor." She turned to Joey for the first time. "Isn't that right, little brother?"

"Right as...snow," Joey said with a grin he didn't need to hide.

"Sit yourselves down," Morton said. "Must be important to bring you all the way from Texas and out on a miserable day like today. Can I get you coffee? Hot chocolate?"

"We're good, thanks." Frank said, speaking for both of them when Joey thought a mug of hot chocolate sounded pretty damned good. He kept his mouth shut. This was Frank's show. He was just along for the ride.

"Mrs. Conrad is concerned about her daughter's whereabouts," Frank said. "Understandably."

"So she brought in the big guns," Morton said.

Frank frowned. "She thought an extra set of eyes might help." He paused. "It's been a couple of weeks without any developments."

Morton nodded. "No one is more frustrated by the lack of progress than me. We can't just make clues up out of thin air, though. They're either there or they aren't. You know what I mean. If no one saw anything, well, no one saw anything. Can't go back in time and place a convenient witness where none exists now."

"Absolutely." He leaned forward. "I assume you've looked at her ex-husband."

Chief Morton slapped her forehead. "Now, why didn't I think of that?" She gave Frank a look that would have sent a lesser man fleeing with his tail between his legs. Joey wished he had popcorn. This was getting good.

"No offence," Frank said, leaning back as if he felt a physical wave of anger emanating from her.

She inhaled deeply, which Joey appreciated. He wished she'd do that a few more times for his benefit. "Luke Stevens has a solid alibi for the time in question. We checked."

Frank put up his hands as a sort of apology, but he didn't allow her to deflect him from his course. "He could have planned that. Paid someone else to do his dirty work."

Morton took another deep breath. "He's not exactly made of money, but it's possible. It's a theory, anyway."

"Have you turned up anything you haven't told the family about?"

"We haven't turned up anything, period. She's just gone. Didn't show up for work, wasn't home, left everything behind, hasn't used a credit card or bought a plane ticket. No sightings, not even false ones. Gone into the Twilight Zone." She shrugged.

"And that doesn't remind you of any other cases?"

She frowned. "What are you getting at?"

"Harvey Andrews."

"Harvey? What about him?"

"He vanished, too, didn't he?"

"That's dementia. Just wandered off. We'll find his body in the spring."

"And the three last year?"

Her face turned red. "Who? What? That was before my time."

Frank counted them on his fingertips. "Eddie Jamieson, last January. Gerald Thompson a month later and Elaine McCarthy a month after that. Last March."

"Before my time, but we don't have open files on them. No one has officially declared them missing, as far as I know." Lauren Morton leaned back in her comfortable-looking chair "So you think we have a serial killer. In Bayport? Isn't that a little far-fetched? This isn't...Houston. Not even Cabot Cove. Where's your proof?"

"I just got here," Frank said. "This is all news to me, too. I only knew about Donna before I arrived."

The police chief shot a dirty look at Joey, who looked away at the framed certificates on the office wall. Morton had a degree in Criminal Justice from Albany, he observed.

"I sure hope you don't plan to turn my town upside down with your wild theories and speculation. Because then we'd have a problem."

Frank held up his hands again. "I'm only here to help out an old friend. I'm not looking to cause any trouble."

"So you will limit yourself to looking into Donna Conrad's disappearance and not go around bothering people with crazy notions about serial killers? I have your word on that?"

"That is my plan, Chief," Frank said.

"Do I have your word on that, Detective?"

Joey watched with pleasure as his brother broke off from the staring contest first. "You do. My word."

"Good. Let me know right away if you turn anything up. And keep in mind that you have no official standing here. Don't overstep your bounds. Got it?"

"Got it."

Lauren summoned Patty and instructed her to make a copy of the investigation file on Donna Conrad for Frank. "You can pick it up later this afternoon," Morton said. "I think it's going to be a quiet day, God willing."

5

"Well, that was fun," Joey said when they were back on Main Street. "What's our next move, Sherlock?"

"I should go see Donna's mother. Let her know I'm in town. Get the keys to Donna's place. Check it out."

"Lead on, McDuff," Joey said.

The storm hadn't let up during their visit with the chief of police. If anything, it seemed to be snowing harder. Hector had made one pass with the plow each way on Main Street, throwing mounds of snow over cars whose owners had the poor judgment to leave them parked on the street, but there was already another inch or two of accumulation on the road surface.

"Shouldn't we call?" Joey asked. "Make sure she's home?"

"Good idea," Frank said.

"I get them now and again."

"You're sure I'm not keeping you from anything important?"

Joey laughed. "Good one, bro."

6

Donna's mother—like most people in Bayport that stormy day, Joey assumed—was home and receiving visitors. She greeted Joey warmly and offered Frank a hug after they had removed their boots in the entryway and hung their parkas on a rack behind the door. Frank seemed uncomfortable at first. In a different world, Joey thought, this might have been his mother-in-law. Donna and his brother had been close for a number of years, and it had been his decision to blow off college and light out for distant lands that had been the end of them. Joey's time with Donna had been much briefer and somewhat fraught with his brother's shadow. He had been constantly aware he didn't quite measure up to Frank in any number of ways.

"What a morning," Mrs. Conrad said. "Cancellations and reschedulings. The storm is making a mess of my calendar."

"It's bad out there," Joey said.

"Thank you for coming, Frank. So good to see you. I'm at my wits' end. I know he did something to her, but no one will listen. Some little missy is giving him an alibi, so he's off the hook, apparently."

"You mean Luke? Her ex-husband."

"Soon-to-be ex," she said. "Donna filed the papers when he was in jail."

"Had she seen him since he got out?"

"I don't know. I don't think so. She was scared of him, so she wasn't likely to meet him alone anywhere. But that doesn't mean he didn't track her down. He's a bad one. We never liked him. Mr. Conrad—my husband, I mean—went to an early grave worried about her."

"Do you remember the last time you saw her?"

"Certainly I do. I've been over that a hundred times, trying to remember anything I might have overlooked. Some clue or sign of trouble. She had an apartment over on Rogers Lane. I wanted her to move in here after she left that…her husband, but she said she wasn't going to be one of those adult children who moved back in with her parents. She had a good job at the marina and wanted to be independent. Free to do things on her own. That's something she didn't have for a long time. Not since he knocked her up."

"So there was nothing out of the ordinary that day, as far as you know."

"She was worried about him, but no more than usual. She stopped by after work for a cup of tea and a chat. She was helping me with the social for the Women's Institute. She'd had a good day—winter is slow at the marina. She stayed until about 6:30, made sure I was going to make myself supper—she was always fussing like that—and then off she went." Mrs. Conrad dabbed the corner of her eye with a handkerchief she had produced like a magician.

"Do you mind if I take a look around her apartment?"

The woman recovered her composure and made the handkerchief disappear again. "I've been trying to decide what to do with the place. Her lease isn't up until the fall, but it seems silly to keep paying for it if she's…"

"I understand," Frank said. "It must be difficult."

"It's the not knowing. Hoping maybe she'll show up tomorrow and everything will go back to normal. But that's not going to happen, is it?" She stood up. "Let me get you the keys."

She went into the kitchen and returned a short while later with a key ring. "This is for the outer door, this is for the apartment, this is for a storage locker in the basement and this is her mailbox key." She looked at Joey. "You know where it is? Of course you do. Your brother was such a help to Donna when she moved."

"Happy I could lend a hand, ma'am," Joey said.

"Do you think you'll find out what happened to her? It was that Luke. I'd bet my bingo winnings on it."

"I'll do my best," Frank said. "If you think of anything or hear anything, you know how to reach me."

"You're staying at your parents' place?"

Frank nodded.

"It's so good that you're back home. It's been too long."

Frank's smile seemed forced, but Joey figured he was accustomed to dealing with the grieving public.

They bundled up to face the storm and headed out to Donna's apartment, three blocks away.

7

"Feels weird, going through someone else's stuff," Joey said.

"You get used to it," Frank said.

They were in Donna's kitchen, examining a stack of papers in a basket on the countertop. Mrs. Conrad must have been picking up her mail, because the box in the lobby was empty except for a grocery store flier containing this week's specials.

"What are we looking for, exactly?"

Frank shrugged. "You never know. You just poke around. Let the place speak to you. If something is odd, it'll stand out."

"Last time I was here, everything was in boxes," Joey said. "Don't you think this whole situation is strange? What kind of person disappears three seemingly random people, then waits a year and does it all over again? That's what you're thinking, right? Someone else is going to vanish soon."

"Maybe," Frank said. "Probably."

"That's fucked up."

"There's always a reason, but it often isn't one an ordinary person can identify with. You know those nut jobs who'll latch onto one thing—a single word in the president's speech for example—and spin an entire wacky conspiracy out of it?"

"I guess."

"Same thing. We had a guy who left his victims' bodies scattered all over the city. One of our techs figured out he was making a picture. When you connected the dots on the map the right way, you got a picture."

"Of what?"

"The constellation Hydra." He saw Joey's reaction. "Didn't make any sense to us, either. But it made sense to him. That's what's important."

"You're the expert."

"I've only had a couple of cases. Serial killers are actually pretty rare."

"Lucky us."

"If that's what we have. There's no proof. All we have are five unrelated incidents."

"And a pattern."

"Maybe," Frank said, sounding less sure than before. "I'm going to check the bedroom. You want to take the bathroom?"

Joey shook his head and picked up the keys. "I think I'll take a look at her storage locker in the basement."

"Okay."

Donna's apartment building was a couple of steps up from a dive, but it had the benefit of strong security doors out front, an important consideration for a battered woman. No elevator, though, so Joey had to tromp down the three flights of stairs he'd carried furniture and boxes up when she'd moved in last fall. He'd been high as a kite that day, he remembered. Donna had kept doing things to make him giggle. It hadn't taken much, and it had removed some of her tension, he thought. This had been more than a move—it had been an escape. A new beginning. He'd offered her a hit off his joint, but she'd declined. "That stuff always makes me sad," she'd said. He'd been self-conscious helping her assemble her bed, but nothing happened there, either.

The basement was dark and dingy, illuminated by flickering fluorescents. It was cold, too. He'd never been down here. When Donna moved in, all of her stuff went into her apartment. She'd said she would take care of storage once she went through everything.

Joey still didn't know what he was looking for, but he knew one thing for certain—the place gave him the creeps. Not only was it cold, it smelled odd. Not the mildewy, stagnant odor one might expect of a dank cellar. It smelled electric, as if a transformer was running hot or lightning had recently struck.

Donna's storage area was more of a cage than a locker. It was made of wire mesh, so anyone could see into it. Her bicycle was hanging by its front wheel from a hook in the ceiling, and a couple of steamer trunks were stacked in one corner, surrounded by a bunch of cardboard boxes. There were wooden pallets on the floor to keep her belongings from getting wet.

He opened the padlock, went in and poked around, but didn't find anything suspicious or helpful. The trunks weren't locked, and he opened them with trepidation, half-expecting to find Donna's body, or worse, body parts within, but they contained only clothing.

He locked the storage unit and spent the next few minutes staring into the adjacent lockers. He continued toward the back corner of the basement, which was dark and poorly lit. He used the flashlight on his cell phone to explore. When the beam glanced across the rear wall, he gasped.

There was a jagged hole through the cement that opened into a long, dark tunnel, like a mineshaft. Cold air emanated from it—bitterly cold air. Disturbingly cold.

He was about to step into the tunnel when he noticed something that freaked him out. The entrance shimmered, as if there was a force field across the opening.

"That's what I smelled," he told himself. "Time to call in reinforcements." He found Frank's number in his recent history and pushed the call button.

"Find something?" Frank asked.

"Uh, maybe. You'd better get down here. And bring a flashlight, if you can find one."

8

Joey returned to the foot of the basement stairs, as far from the unusual hole in the wall as possible, while he waited for his brother to descend from the third-floor apartment. The tunnel made him uneasy.

"What's the big emergency?" Frank asked when he arrived a few minutes later.

"Sorry to pull you away from pawing through Donna's unmentionables," Joey said, "but I wondered how this fits into your theory of the crime?"

"Theory of the crime?"

"I watch TV," Joey said with a nervous laugh. "I know the lingo." He led his brother around the storage cages to the back wall. He took the flashlight from him and shone the beam on the opening.

"What am I supposed to be looking for?" Frank asked, peering at the tunnel. He put his hands on his thighs and bent over.

"The hole," Joey said. "Duh."

"What hole?"

Joey gaped. He turned to see if Frank was teasing him. His brother looked confused more than anything. Frank reached out and ran his hand over the wall—or, rather over the opening to the tunnel.

"You can't see it? Or feel it? A hole big enough to drive a tank through."

"Are you tripping?" Frank asked. "Did you take something after you came down here?"

Joey wondered if he was suffering a flashback from yesterday's acid trip. He'd heard such things were possible, but he'd never believed it. He took out his phone and opened the camera app. After snapping a couple of pictures, he held the camera up so his brother could see the display.

"It's a very nice wall, as basement walls go," Frank said.

"Fuck," Joey said. "What's going on?" As much as he didn't want to, he reached for the wall. He half expected to encounter resistance when his palm met the shimmering patch, but his hand passed into the opening. The hair on his arm stood up, and his skin tingled. It was several degrees colder on the other side.

"What the fuck?" Frank said, pulling Joey back. "How did you do that?"

"I told you. There's a hole."

"Do it again. I'm watching you closely, so no tricks."

Joey didn't really want to put his hand into that creepy place again, but he needed to convince his brother he wasn't high. Or insane. Or both. He repeated the gesture, slowly this time, standing so Frank had an unobstructed view. The tingling sensation wasn't unpleasant, but it was disturbing.

"Jesus Christ," Frank said. "That's the weirdest fucking thing I've ever seen." He reached out again. When his hand made contact with the force field, it stopped. He ran his palm over the surface, then rapped on the wall with his knuckles.

THE DEAD OF WINTER

Joey could hear the sound, though it looked like Frank was knocking on thin air. "How come I can't feel or see it?" Frank asked. He took a deep breath and for several seconds seemed lost in thought. He stepped back and stared at the wall. "And what does it have to do with Donna's disappearance?"

"It has to be connected," Joey said. "I mean, come on. How could it not be? Suppose she found this tunnel and went into it and couldn't get back out."

"Doesn't explain why I can't see it."

Joey shrugged. "Suppose it's only meant for certain people."

"That has to be the craziest thing I've ever heard."

"Maybe so, but how else do you explain this?" He held his breath and stuck his hand into the hole, all the way to his elbow.

"Stop that," Frank said. "You're messing with my head." He kicked the wall. It certainly sounded solid to Joey's ears. "Tell me what you see."

"A tunnel. Goes on as far as I can see. Maybe if we had a better light..."

Frank didn't say anything.

"What are you thinking?"

"A couple things."

"I'll bet number one is: How can I convince Joey to go in there and look around."

Frank's grin lacked all humor. "No. I was wondering if there's a tunnel like this in the basements of the other people who vanished. Maybe they're all connected."

Joey snorted. "Wow. That's a pretty big leap. We just encountered the most batshit crazy thing either one of us has ever seen, and now you're guessing there are more of them?"

Frank shrugged. "It's a theory. Easily tested."

Joey scrunched up his mouth while he considered what his brother was saying. "What else?"

"I was wondering what it means that you can see the tunnel and I can't. What does that say about you?"

"That I'm special."

Frank chewed on the inside of his mouth. "Maybe the people who vanished were lured into tunnels like these."

"These hypothetical other tunnels," Joey said. Then the full impact of what his brother meant struck him. "So you're saying..."

"I'm saying—maybe you're supposed to be Mr. March."

9

On the way back to the house, they stopped at Quiznos and grabbed a couple of club sandwiches and a pot of chili for lunch. The owner, though glad to see them, said she was reconsidering her decision to open. None of her employees had shown up for work, and very few customers were likely to brave the weather. The wind had picked up in the past hour or so, and the snow was drifting almost horizontally.

After Joey reheated the chili on the stove, they ate in stunned silence while they contemplated the morning's events. When they were done, they washed up, including the heaps of older dishes cluttering the sink and surrounding counters. Then Joey gathered the empty beer bottles and the pizza boxes and took them to the back porch for recycling. He felt like they were stalling, unwilling to take the next step.

When they were finished, Joey asked, "What now?"

Frank looked at his cell phone. "We could wait until tomorrow, but it doesn't look like the storm is going to let up anytime soon."

"Wait for what?"

"To check out the other places."

"For tunnels."

"No matter how unlikely..."

Joey frowned.

"You called me Sherlock earlier. I can't eliminate the existence of an impossible tunnel only you can see. No matter how unlikely it seems."

"Im-fucking-possible, you mean," Joey said. "But if what you said about me being next is true..."

"I don't know that. It's just a guess."

"So, shouldn't we check out our own cellar, first? Before we go back out in that shit?"

Frank started. "I should have thought of that."

"Put your eyes back in your head. I told you I get an idea every now and then."

"You have a better flashlight than the one in your cell phone?"

"Somewhere," Joey said. He rummaged around in a cabinet and came up with a four-cell flashlight. When he clicked the button, the bulb produced a feeble yellow glow for a few seconds, then dimmed and went out. In a basket on top of the fridge, he turned up a fresh set of batteries and they were good to go.

THE DEAD OF WINTER

Joey couldn't remember when he'd last been downstairs. During the time he'd been living in the place alone, his universe had shrunk. Most nights he didn't make it upstairs to his old bedroom, falling asleep on the couch in front of the TV and game console.

As they rounded the corner beside the furnace, Joey stumbled into something and almost fell. When he regained his footing, he realized what had tripped him up. Now he remembered putting the winter tires down here the previous spring, where they'd be out of the way. He shook his head at his forgetfulness. Must be the drugs, he told himself.

They checked out every corner of the cellar, but didn't find anything unusual. Frank wasn't of much help, because he wasn't likely to be able to see a tunnel, assuming one existed to be seen. Joey shook his head. He'd done some crazy things in his life, but this just about topped them all.

"What now?" Joey asked once they were satisfied there was nothing to be found.

"Mr. Andrews disappeared before Donna. Where does he live?"

Joey thought for a second. "Over on Pleasant View."

"Think we'd be able to get in?"

"You mean, like, break in?"

Frank didn't answer.

"Don't you cops carry lock-picking shit?"

Frank smirked. "You watch too much TV. What about you? Don't you druggies have B&E gear?"

"Touché," Joey said. He looked around the basement. "There are probably some things down here we can use. It's not like anyone's likely to see us on a day like today. Chief Morton'll blow a gasket if she finds out, though. You promised to focus on Donna."

"I go where the evidence leads," Frank said.

"Try explaining an invisible hole to her," he said. "I'd like to see that."

10

Joey threw open the garage doors to reveal the Arctic Cat snowmobile he'd purchased three years earlier, when work was steadier. It wasn't completely paid for yet, but he'd gotten good use out of it. The field behind the house was surrounded by woods where he'd created a series of trails in recent winters. He'd already had it out several times this year, so it was ready to go.

"Why didn't you mention this earlier?" Frank asked.

Joey grinned and pulled his goggles over his eyes before keying the machine to life. He carefully skirted the snow-covered mound in the driveway that was his Civic, and set off down the street with Frank riding bitch. They had the road pretty much to themselves, and all evidence of their passage would soon be eradicated by the storm or the plow.

When they reached the Andrews place, Joey took a run at the bank at the end of the driveway, nearly unseating Frank in the process, and pulled up at the back door, out of sight of prying neighbors.

"Doesn't look like anyone's home," Frank said after the snowmobile engine fell silent.

"I don't think his kids stayed long. Busy lives in other parts. You know how it is," Joey said. "I imagine they let Theresa go. Not much point looking after the place when the owner's gone walkabout. We'll see a Fitzpatrick Realty sign out front come spring and maybe in a year or two it'll sell."

Frank tested the knob on the back door to make sure it was locked before he set to work with the tools they'd rounded up from their father's workshop. The cold made his hand shake, but it didn't take him long to get it open. They stomped the snow off their boots before going inside and closing the door behind them.

The house was warm enough for them to loosen their scarves but cold enough that they kept their jackets on. A patina of dust covered everything. It didn't take long for a place to look like it had been abandoned, Joey thought. Ashes and dust. After their father died, he'd been afraid Frank would insist they sell and split the proceeds. There was no way he would've been able to buy Frank out, even on the installment plan, so he'd been secretly pleased to discover his brother was still nostalgic about a place he'd fled at the first available opportunity.

He ran his fingers along the piano keys as he walked past, creating an eerie soundtrack to their incursion. Breaking and entering with his brother hadn't been on his bucket list and yet here they were. "Basement?" he suggested when his brother glanced at him.

Frank nodded.

THE DEAD OF WINTER

In the kitchen, they found a door leading to the cellar. There was a step-on garbage can at the top of the stairs and a cubbyhole that served as a mini-pantry overhead about halfway down. Apparently Professor Andrews had been a fan of sugary cereals, the kind Joey had enjoyed as a child. When was the last time he'd had a bowl of Cap'n Crunch?

Holding the flashlight, Frank led the way. At the bottom, he scanned first left, then right. Against the far wall was a 275-gallon tank for furnace oil. The laundry room doubled as a storage room for pickled vegetables and super-sized packages from Costco. There was enough toilet paper stacked up to last a decade.

Around the corner, they found a messy workbench strewn with never-to-be-completed projects. In a rotating rack hanging from the ceiling, screws, nuts and bolts were stored in jam and pickle jars of various shapes. The professor had been organized about some things but others, not so much.

At the rear of the cellar, they found a door that presumably opened onto a set of stairs leading up to the back yard, stairs that were undoubtedly buried in snow at the moment.

"See anything?" Frank asked.

Joey shook his head. He'd momentarily forgotten he was the only one who'd be able to find anything unusual. He was already beginning to doubt what they'd seen in Donna's basement, and he had no plans to look at the photo on his cell phone to reassure himself it had really happened.

Frank swept the beam across the wall on the far side of the furnace, and there it was. Joey's mouth went dry and his heart raced. He blinked, slowly, hoping that when he opened his eyes, it would be gone.

By then, the flashlight beam had moved on and Joey was tempted to let it slide. It was, after all, full-bore crazy, this thing they were doing. But he couldn't unsee it. "Stop," he said, his voice overloud in the confined space. "Go back."

Frank retraced the section of wall he'd just illuminated with the flashlight. "Say when."

"When," Joey said.

The opening in the wall resembled the one in Donna's basement. It was at least six feet across and jagged around the edges, as if it had been caused by some kind of explosion. The tunnel continued for as far as Joey could see, which wasn't all that far. An eerie cold breeze wafted out of the opening and Joey once again detected the strange electrical odor he'd noticed earlier.

"Smell that?"

Frank took a deep breath and shook his head.

"Gimme," Joey said, snatching the flashlight from his brother's hand. He aimed the light at the wall at an oblique angle. That odd, shimmering pattern across the entrance was here, too.

"Tell me," Frank said.

"Same as at Donna's." He described what he was seeing, spreading his arms to show how big the hole was. Frank rapped on solid concrete, but Joey was once again able to reach into the tunnel to prove what he was seeing.

Frank checked his watch. "We probably shouldn't stay here too long, in case someone notices the snowmobile in the backyard. We can't count on the storm keeping everyone inside."

Joey nodded. "Just a sec," he said, and used his cell phone to take several pictures. "For future reference," he said. He looked at his brother. "You don't want me to go in there, right? I mean, I'd definitely want a couple of stiff drinks first."

Frank frowned. "At some point we're probably going to have to go in there, but not yet."

"We, huh? How are 'we' going to get in there if only I can see it, huh? Tell me that, Kemo Sabe."

Frank held up his hands. "I know. I know. We'll figure that out when the time comes. Let's get out of here."

11

The shelves at the grocery store were starting to look a little on the sparse side when they stopped to get supplies on the way back home, and there'd been a run on booze at the package store down the block. The residents of Bayport knew how to ride out a storm. Joey and Frank grabbed a couple of cases of beer and a few bottles of liquor from the dwindling stock.

At the checkout, the clerk peered at Frank, who still had his wool hat on, pulled over his ears, and his scarf puddled around his chin. "I know you. You're that Shaw fella. Played football a while back." The clerk looked to be nearly seventy.

Joey was curious to see if his brother would fess up.

"Yeah, I used to play some," Frank said.

THE DEAD OF WINTER

The man nodded, apparently satisfied that his memory was still reliable, and completed the transaction. "You boys be careful out there," he said after their purchases were bagged. "This is going to get a lot worse before it gets better."

On the way back to the house, the brothers detoured to the police station to pick up Chief Morton's file on Donna Conrad. The chief was out, and Patty wasn't in a talkative mood, so it was a brief stop.

The day's adventures and being out in the storm had left them famished. After they stowed the snowmobile, they set about cooking supper and drinking beer. It had taken Joey less than twenty-four hours to break his resolve. Fuck it, he thought. After what they'd been through, even a Buddhist monk would want to get soused.

"At least the power's still on," Joey said.

"Shh," Frank said. "Don't jinx us."

Joey turned the thermostat up to 75, far warmer than he normally kept the house. He was having a hard time shaking the chill that had settled upon him. It was more than the cold weather. It was the undeniable realization that something that defied all explanation was happening. He'd felt bad when Donna vanished, worried, like her mother, that her ex had done something to her. But now...

"You wanna turn those things over before they burn?" Frank asked, interrupting his reverie.

Joey grimaced and flipped the burgers. "Sorry," he said. "Lost in thought."

"It's a lot to take in," Frank said as he pulled the fries from the boiling oil and spread them out on paper towels to soak up the excess. He'd already laid out the buns and cheese slices on plates near the stove.

"What could create a tunnel like that in the first place, let alone do that hocus pocus thing with the entrance?"

Frank shook his head and dumped the fries onto side plates.

"I mean, it's more than hidden," Joey said, flipping the burgers one last time. "As far as you're concerned, it's not there at all."

"Good thing you checked Donna's basement," Frank said.

It was the nicest thing his brother had said to him in recent memory. Almost a compliment. He decided not to make a fuss over it. Let it slide. He scooped the burgers onto the open buns, dumped the frying pan into the dishpan in the sink and grabbed the plates. Frank took care of the fries and brought fresh bottles of beer from the fridge.

"Think we should check out the other places?" Joey asked through a mouthful of burger.

"I've been giving that some thought," Frank said. "Not right away, at least. Better not push our luck with the illegal activities. Besides, if we found the same thing there, we wouldn't have any new information."

Frank wiped his mouth on a paper towel, the closest thing they had to napkins without breaking out their mother's old fine linens.

"I've been thinking, too. About something you said earlier," Joey said.

"What's that?"

"About that guy and his constellation design. Could there be a pattern here, too—to where the tunnels are located?"

"Huh. You're on a roll, brother. I'll make a cop out of you yet. Do you have a town map?"

"I can print one out later," Joey said.

They ate in silence for a while. Joey was the first to speak. "I can't get over the scope of the tunnel. Digging something like that is a major undertaking. It'd take a full crew with tons of equipment. How does no one notice? And what do you do with all the stuff you dug up?"

Frank nodded. "All good questions. I have no answers."

Frank *always* had answers, in Joey's experience, so this admission must have been difficult. He was working on the beer bottle label again, Joey noticed, but he wasn't doing his usual neat job. It was tearing around the edges. "I wonder if anything like this has ever happened before. Anywhere. All sorts of crazy shit gets reported—most of it amounts to nothing, but this? The people who try to talk about it are written off as lunatics. But you and I *know* this is real."

"Depends on your definition of real," Joey said. He was quiet for a while. "Maybe it was the acid."

"Huh?"

"I kinda sorta took a trip yesterday before you got here. Maybe that consciousness raising experience put me in the right frame of mind to see the tunnels." Joey could read the disapproval in his brother's face. "You should try it sometime," Joey said. "Let your hair down, what little of what you have left. Is that the HPD regulation cut?"

Frank polished off his beer and set the bottle aside with one of the labels intact.

THE DEAD OF WINTER

"It's possible, isn't it?" Joey said. "I mean, come on. We're talking about crazy shit here. Nothing is off the table, right?"

"I guess. Maybe the effect will wear off, if that's the case."

"I can always get more," Joey said.

"I'll bet."

"Or not. Anyway, getting back to your initial question. How do we find out if this has happened before?"

"Research," Frank said. "I assume you have a computer? Connected to the internet? Everything winds up on the 'net eventually."

Joey wrinkled his nose. "I have color TV, too. Yee-haw."

"Okay. Let's clean up and hit the books."

Once everything was washed, dried and put back where it belonged, Joey said, "You're going to make someone a good housewife someday."

Frank smiled. It was tinged with sadness—their mother used to say the same thing to them when they were kids and helped with the chores.

"I'll print that town map first," Joey said.

"Big as you can," Frank said.

"Roger that."

While Frank leafed through Morton's file on Donna's disappearance, Joey printed half a dozen sheets of paper and taped them together to create a map nearly two feet on a side. It showed the crescent shape of the town. The main road leading into Bayport was a spur off Route 24 that curled around the coastline before circling back to meet itself. Only the lower half of the loop was populated. The northern side was swampland.

Joey cleared the kitchen table and flattened the map, then pinpointed the homes of the five missing people with a black marker. When he was finished, he stood back.

"What you got?" Frank asked.

"Nothing," Joey said. "No pattern. Not a straight line or a square, at least. Could be just about anything. Gemini or Sagittarius, for all I know."

"Let me see." Frank came over to the table. He stared at the map for a while. Then he took the marker and went over the dots Joey had made until they were nearly half an inch across.

"Much better," Joey said. "I see it now."

Frank ignored his brother's sarcastic tone and flipped the map over. The dots were clearly visible through the printer paper. "Patience, grasshopper," he said. He took a pen from his pocket and drew a light line connecting two dots and then another to join two more.

"A cock-eyed star?" Joey asked.

"I'm mostly interested in the vertex," Frank said. "The hub of activity. It's not the same distance to each dot, but it is in the middle of things. What's there?"

Joey grabbed the marker and blackened in the intersection point, then flipped the map over again. His dot was in the middle of the swamp around the mill pond.

"Interestink," he said in his best Sgt. Schultz accent.

12

Finding nothing useful in the police report, Frank hit the computer and started reading old newspaper articles and visiting conspiracy theory websites featuring reports of UFO sightings and other strange occurrences. Joey got bored after a while and powered up the game console. He felt the urge to shoot something and *World War Z* was just the game to scratch that itch.

He was still at it when Frank shut the computer down a couple of hours later and strolled over to sit beside him on the couch. At a break in the action, Joey handed over the controller. "Want to take a shot?" He figured his brother would refuse, but Frank surprised him.

"Sure," Frank said. He entered the fray and spent the next fifteen minutes shooting, stabbing and beheading zombies. He showed no hesitation, and his marksmanship was impressive. As far as Joey could tell, every shot was a kill shot.

"We should go to the firing range sometime," Joey said.

"Think you could keep up?"

Joey laughed. "Probably not. But it would be fun trying." When Frank handed the controller back, Joey used it to shut the system down. "I'm whipped," he said. He paused. "I was thinking about sparking up a joint. Take the edge off. You won't turn me in to your old girlfriend, will you?"

Frank frowned, but Joey knew he knew who he was talking about.

"Come on. Don't pretend you and the new police chief didn't knock boots a few times back in the day."

Frank opened and closed his mouth. "You knew?"

"Dude. Everyone knew."

THE DEAD OF WINTER

Frank processed that. "Everyone?"
"Well, not Mom and Dad, maybe, but everyone at school."
Frank swallowed. "Donna?"
Joey nodded.
"Shit. She never said anything."
"Not one of your finer hours, but all the guys were impressed. Banging two hot chicks at the same time, one of them a cheerleader and the other the future homecoming queen."
"Man. No wonder things went the way they did."
"What do you mean?"
"Get that joint and I'll tell you."
It was Joey's turn to be surprised. His normally straight-laced brother had hidden depths.
After they shared the joint, they settled down in the living room with the rest of the beers and a stack of snack food from their shopping run. Joey sat in the easy chair where their mother used to watch "her shows" and knit, while Frank stretched out on the sofa. The air around them was blue with smoke, reminding Joey of the time an old girlfriend had dropped in to his apartment unannounced. He and his pals were stoned out of their gourds, and all he could think to do was wave his arms in the air and say, "Craziest fucking thing happened—the couch caught fire!" He hadn't fooled the friend, he knew, and she hadn't stayed long.
Frank grabbed a handful of chips and ate them one after the other without break. He repeated the process before starting his story. "Forgot how hungry that shit makes me," he said. "I was never going to be another Jerry Rice or Randy Moss, no matter how good everyone told me I was. I was fast but not that fast, and I could get my hands on a ball if it was in my neighborhood, but nothing special. Just about good enough for a full ride scholarship. Who knows? Maybe even good enough to get drafted. If I survived, that is. I took some solid hits, both in practice and during games. And this was only high school, where the players were relatively small. A couple of times after I got my bell rung, I couldn't remember what happened for the next five or ten minutes. I was on my feet and doing stuff, running the plays, but I was like a robot. Or a zombie."
"Shit, man," Joey said.
"At least I wasn't a linebacker. Those guys took it almost every play. Plus, the coach wanted them to bulk up, so some of them were juicing, and that crap does bad things to a man's body—a boy's body, really."

Joey took a swig of beer. He was feeling amazingly mellow, despite everything.

"So I started doing crazy shit. Like Lauren Franklin. She was hell on wheels, back then. Live as a firecracker and as touchy as nitroglycerin. We didn't last long together but it was intense."

"Chief Morton. Do tell."

"She rocks that uniform, am I right?"

"Yes, indeedy," Joey said. "I have newfound respect for the office. Mad respect."

"There was some other crazy stuff. I don't remember half of it. Coke and pills."

"You? Frank Almighty, the king of Bayport High?"

"You can get away with a lot when you're at the top of the heap," Frank said. "People look the other way, especially when you're winning, and we won a lot."

"I remember."

"So, senior year, while we're fielding offers from universities, with people telling me on the sly they had ways of making sure I kept up the necessary grades, and all of us knowing what they meant, and me getting my brain rattled on a regular basis, something happened."

"What?" Joey asked.

"Hard to explain," Frank said. He grabbed another handful of chips and crammed them into his mouth. "These are *so* good." He wiped his hands on his pants. "Where was I? Oh yeah. So it was like an epiphany, you know, one of those sudden awakenings. I was on this freight train that was building up a head of steam and unstoppable momentum, and all of a sudden I wanted off. Except..."

"Except the conductor wouldn't let you."

"Exactly," Frank said. "Exactly. The fucking conductor, the engineer, the guy stoking the engine, everyone wanted this train to keep on chugging along. Dad got pissed if I so much as suggested I didn't want to play football at university. He had a spot cleared off on top of the piano for the eventual Heisman Trophy. He didn't get to go to university, so I think he was kinda living vicariously through me."

"So that train wasn't stopping."

"No way, no how. The drugs were my way of trying to derail it I guess. Women, too. I was probably hoping to impregnate someone so I'd have a good excuse to drop out. So I spread my seed far and wide."

"Ewww," Joey said. Then he started giggling and couldn't stop. That got Frank laughing and it took them a while to get under control.

"Good shit," Frank said, and that started them laughing again. "Anyway, the joke was on me, because it turned out I was shooting blanks. Didn't find that out until Melissa and I tried to have kids. One more nail in the coffin, that was."

Joey was tempted to say he was sorry, but he was also on the verge of another giggling fit, picturing Frank like a gunslinger armed only with a cap gun. Instead he took another swig of beer and grabbed a handful of cheese puffs. There was something fascinating about their fluorescent orange color and the way they filled his mouth with flavor, but he always managed to get them impacted into one of his wisdom teeth.

"So that's when I decided I had to get away from all this. If I went to college and played football, I knew I was going to get hurt, perhaps seriously, and I probably wasn't going to get much of an education. A degree, maybe, but a useless one. So once the football was gone, where would I be?"

"Up shit creek," Joey said, licking orange powder from his fingertips.

"Paddle-free," Frank said.

"Why Houston?" Joey asked.

"There was probably a good reason at the time, but I don't remember it now. Something to do with a girl, most likely. Not all of my decisions at the time were rational. I sat down with Mom and Dad one evening—"

"I remember that. You talked to Mom first and then Dad got called in."

"I think they thought I'd gotten Donna pregnant. Mom was relieved. Dad was furious when I told him my plans. He held it together—he was getting some serious silent communication from Mom—but I could tell. Not sure he ever got over it."

"I think he did," Joey said. "Until the dementia set in. Then he started reliving a lot of that. You're right—he was mad at you."

"He didn't come around the day I left. You either, as I recall."

"I was off getting my ass kicked, as *I* recall."

"What?"

"Dad wasn't the only one who was mad at you for leaving. Some guys decided to take it out on me. You know teenagers. Their logical thinking skills are impaired by their hormones."

"Ha!" Frank said.

"What?"

"You said 'hormone!'" They giggled some more, but not as long this time. "Seriously, though. People got mad at you because I left?"

"For a while. A lot of feelings and not many outlets for them."

"Sorry you had to go through that," Frank said.

Joey shrugged, then nodded to acknowledge the apology. "How'd you wind up on the police force?"

Frank pulled a face as if to say, "How the hell do I know?"

"Come on. You don't accidentally become a cop."

"I kinda did. They were actively recruiting when I got there. Went to an information night at the Academy and signed up then and there. Worked part-time jobs to support myself, but Houston can be a cheap place to live if you do it right."

Joey shook his head. "I couldn't take the heat."

Frank laughed. "A lot better than this shit," he said. "You don't have to shovel sunshine. The bugs, now that's an entirely different matter. Big suckers that can fly."

"Texas sized," Joey said.

"You got that right."

"I half expected you to be wearing a ten-gallon hat and boots when I picked you up."

"I know a few people who do, but not many."

They fell silent for a while. Frank resumed picking at the label of his beer bottle. The peak high had passed and now Joey just felt tired. "I'm going to have to go into one of those tunnels, aren't I?"

Frank didn't say anything for a while. "First, there's someone we need to talk to," he said.

"Who?"

"Someone who can tell us about the mill pond and the swamp," Frank said.

13

The power went out during the night. Something clicked when it did, a subtle sound that was barely loud enough to wake Joey up. The first thing he noticed was that the red light that normally glowed on the front of his game console when it was hibernating was off. He flipped the light switch next to the couch to confirm his suspicion.

He put on his parka and boots and took the big flashlight with him when he went out to the back deck to start the

THE DEAD OF WINTER

generator his father had installed the year after the harsh winter of 1998. "A day late and a dollar short," their mother had said on more than one occasion whenever the subject of the generator came up, but it had proved useful over the years.

Joey didn't need to worry about the furnace—it ran on stove oil and the tank was nearly full—but the blowers that circulated the warm air were electric. The generator also kept the hot water heater and the fridge running.

He plugged the TV into the one extra power outlet the generator supplied to check the weather. He could have used the app on his phone, but he had a thing for the redhead on the Weather Channel. She could have forecast the coming apocalypse and it would have sounded fine to him.

It wasn't far from that, according to their report. They didn't use words like "snowpocalypse" or "snowmageddon," like the more sensationalist stations, but it amounted to much the same thing. The National Weather Service had given the blizzard a name—Bruno—which was never a good sign. Apparently the worst was yet to come, and the mayors of the major cities in the region were declaring emergencies and shutting the roads. Coastal surges and flooding were possible, as well as record-breaking snowfall amounts. Joey's favorite forecaster wasn't anywhere to be found, though, so once he had the gist of the situation, he switched the TV off and started to think about breakfast.

He connected the coffee machine to the live outlet and set a large pot to brew. Then he drank three glasses of water to get rid of the cotton mouth he always experienced after a night like last night. It wasn't yet six AM, but he was wide awake. He moved about quietly so as not to awaken his brother, whom he assumed was asleep upstairs.

According to the power company, someone had already reported the outage. "Service will be restored in *.* hours," the website announced, which wasn't encouraging. It sounded like the digital equivalent of "fuck knows."

Presumably lured downstairs by the smell of coffee, Frank came into the kitchen, scratching his belly and yawning. "Power's out," he said.

"No shit, Sherlock," Joey said.

"Generator still works, I see."

"Day late," Joey said.

"And a dollar short. Ha! I haven't thought about that in a long time."

"His name is Bruno," Joey said.

"Who? The generator?"

Joey waved his hand in the general direction of the howling winds. "No, dumbass. The storm. We're due for a metric fuckton of snow, and Cat. 5 winds."

"Why did I ever leave Houston?" Frank asked.

"Hope they aren't expecting you back soon."

"My lieutenant's going to laugh when I tell him I can't report for work on account of snow. Exactly how much is a metric fuckton?"

"Ten shitloads," Joey said, looking through the window into the backyard. "It's metric."

It was past time for the sun to start coming up, but it was hard to tell through the heavy gray clouds and the steady snowfall. It was going to be days before everything got back to normal—perhaps as much as a week. No skin off his nose—he had nothing going on to be disrupted by the weather. If he couldn't get anywhere for a few days, he wouldn't be inconvenienced.

They rustled up breakfast using a combination of small electrical appliances and the Coleman camp stove. Lighting it indoors probably wasn't the wisest move, but it was only for a short while. After they cleaned up, they put on their outdoor gear and got ready to face the blizzard once more.

14

Charlie Benson was a local character. He was at least seventy, although to Joey he'd always seemed old. If he ever stood up straight, he probably would have been over six feet tall, but his back was perpetually hunched. He weighed at least 300 pounds, was generally poorly shaved and reeked. His breath always smelled of alcohol, if you were brave enough to get close enough to detect it. Their parents used to say he'd been good at some subjects in school, but he was dull-witted now. Good-natured most of the time, even when drunk. He had a phlegmatic laugh that was contagious, even though it sounded like he was on the verge of pneumonia.

Technically, Charlie was a squatter. He lived in a tiny place on the edge of the swamp, but he didn't own the land. Apparently no one knew who did. It was an ideal place for him, and for the town. He could be part of the community and apart from it at the same time.

Residents of Bayport treated him like a pet project. Took him clothes and meals, bought him groceries, drove him home—especially after an overindulgent evening at Sal's—and generally kept an eye out. Younger people took advantage of him because he was generous to a fault and an easy mark, especially when it came to alcohol, which was the only thing he ever seemed to buy for himself. When he was paid for an odd job, some locals took him straight to the grocery store to make sure he spent the money on food, although he was known to fill his cart with inexpensive bulky items like bread and cereal to make it look like he'd purchased a lot, saving most of the cash for cheap whiskey.

His eyesore of a house was hand-painted in uneven horizontal purple and blue stripes, and the interior smelled of cat piss, on account of the fact that he had at least a dozen of them living with him at any given time. Joey's parents had often dispatched him or Frank to Charlie's with sweaters and heavy socks knitted by the local women, or with food left over from social events. Joey always held his breath when he got to the door, and tried to spend as little time inside as possible. He hadn't been there in years.

And here they were again, about to head over to Charlie's place. As Joey was opening the back porch door, Frank said, "Do you think we should take him something? Food or...?"

"I think we should hang on to what little we have. If this storm keeps up, we're going to need it. I don't want to have to sleep with one eye open, wondering if you're planning to kill and eat me."

"Pretty funny."

"I'll throw a few cans into a sack," Joey said.

It took them a while to get the garage open. Joey wasn't great at estimating things, but he guessed there were at least two feet of snow in front of the doors. Some of it had drifted there, but an impressive amount had come down overnight.

Finally, sweating in their heavy outfits as if they'd spent an hour at the gym, they were underway with the gas tank topped off and a jerry can strapped to the back of the Arctic Cat.

The streets of Bayport were deserted. Nothing was open, and it looked like the power was out all over town. They passed a few people trying to open their driveways or at least get the porch steps shoveled off, and Hector had been out with the plow, but the streets were still snow-packed, which made it good going for the snowmobile.

"On the way back home, we should stop in and liberate some food from the grocery store," Joey yelled. "Before it goes bad."

"What?" Frank yelled back.

Joey shook his head and gunned the engine, taking advantage of the straightaway to open the machine up, see what it could do. He was going sixty when he blew past the police station.

The closer Joey brought the Arctic Cat to Charlie's place, and the swamp beyond, the worse the road conditions grew, until it became hard to tell exactly where the road was. He used telephone poles for navigation. It wouldn't do to go too far astray and risk passing over a partly frozen section of open water. Hardly a winter went by without at least one snowmobiler falling through the ice, usually with fatal results.

There had never been a mill at the mill pond in Joey's lifetime, but the place had a reputation. Parents warned their children to stay away from the swampy area surrounding it. There were patches of quicksand, they said, which could swallow a person whole. They'd never be heard of again and no one would know what transpired, unless someone happened to find a hat floating on the surface, a vivid image that had stayed with Joey. He'd watched enough adventure movies to be petrified of quicksand. A standup comic he'd seen on TV once observed, "When I was growing up, I always thought quicksand would be a much bigger problem than it actually is," and Joey had nodded in agreement. He still had nightmares about being buried up to his chest in the thick brown goop, sinking inch by inch until it reached his neck, at which point he normally woke up, bathed in sweat.

When they reached Charlie's place, they saw gray-brown smoke rising from behind an enormous snowdrift. It looked like Charlie was home and burning whatever he could get his hands on to stay warm. Joey glanced over his shoulder to make sure Frank was holding onto the side rails, then aimed the Arctic Cat at the drift covering the spot where the entrance to Charlie's yard was most likely located. The snowmobile took flight, landing solidly in the open field on the other side. Joey had to do some fancy maneuvering to avoid a pair of trash barrels sticking out of the snowbank before pulling up in front of the varicolored house. He waited for Frank to make a crack about his driving skills, but his brother was looking instead

THE DEAD OF WINTER

at Charlie's front door. No doubt imagining the way it would smell once they were inside, especially in the heat generated by his wood stove.

People rarely stood on ceremony by knocking on Charlie's front door, which opened into what would have been a front porch in most houses. Except for a narrow path leading to the inner door, every square inch was filled with piles of old furniture and other cast-offs.

Frank carried the plastic bag filled with canned food as a kind of offering. Joey hoped they wouldn't regret this generosity. He had only been half joking about raiding the grocery store on the way home. If this storm kept up, the food situation could get dire. When he'd looked at the weather earlier, he saw that Bayport was getting the worst of it by far, and he doubted anyone in the surrounding areas knew how bad it was here. The town wasn't a passing-through point; it was a terminus. If you didn't have business in Bayport, you wouldn't end up here, even by accident.

Frank pushed open the door between the porch and the house. Charlie was sitting at a small, rickety table. Off to one side was his bed, covered with cats. On the other side was a cramped kitchen with an old icebox and an even older wood-fire stove. There had to be a bathroom somewhere, but Joey had never seen it, nor did he want to. Not for a million dollars.

"We brought you something," Frank said, putting the bag on the table.

Charlie never ever acknowledged the acts of generosity bestowed upon him by the community, but whether it was out of obliviousness or embarrassment Joey didn't know. He took a swing of amber liquid from a water glass. "I know you?" he asked, then wheezed that peculiar laugh of his. Then he looked at Joey. "You, I know." Then he looked back at Frank, as if piecing the clues together. "Okay. I remember now."

"Quite a storm," Joey said, making idle conversation.

Charlie took another hit from the glass. "Anything to drink in there?" He pulled the plastic bag open with a grubby finger and wheezed another laugh. "Don't suppose so. Never is."

Joey reached into an inner pocket and produced a pint of scotch he'd grabbed before they set out that morning. Charlie's eyes fixed on the bottle the way a cat watches the red dot of a laser beam.

"Mind if we sit for a minute?" Joey asked, wondering when the last time was that anyone had volunteered to stay a second longer than necessary.

Charlie kicked the chairs across from him out and grunted. The brothers took this as an invitation to sit. It was crowded around the tiny table, and the fact that three cats decided to join them, nosing around the grocery bag, didn't help. There were several others on the floor, slinking between their feet and scratching at the wooden chair legs.

Charlie drained his glass and half filled it with the scotch. He didn't offer to share. "You back in town?" he asked, wiping his lips and sighing. Joey figured the good stuff was wasted on the man, but as long as he appreciated it, so what?

"For a few days," Frank said. "Until the storm is over."

Charlie wheezed and then started coughing. When he finished, he spit into a brownish handkerchief that had probably been white once upon a time and stuffed it back into his pants pocket. At least he was wearing pants—that wasn't always the case, in Joey's experience. "Better get comfortable, then," Charlie said. "Could be a while."

Joey knew Charlie didn't have a TV, and he doubted the man had a cell phone, either. He would've lost it by now, or sold it to buy booze. "You been watching the Weather Channel, Charlie?"

The older man wiped his fingers across his lips and wheezed some more. His face was bright red and sweat dotted his brow. "Heh, heh, heh." He wiped his forehead with the back of his hand. "Don't need no Tee Vee to know that."

"The reason we're here," Frank said, "is to ask you about the swamp. Have you ever heard any stories about it?"

Charlie wiped his mouth again and broke into another breathless round of laughter. "You mean like...ghost stories?" He put his thumbs to his ears and waggled his fingers. "Boogie man, heh, heh?" He stuck his hands out toward Frank and wiggled his fingers some more. "Marie Laveau, boogadee, boogadee?" He laughed so hard he had to stop and spit some more phlegm into his handkerchief.

One of the cats on the table hissed and leapt past Joey to the bed. "This was a waste of time," he said to his brother. "Enjoy the food, Charlie. Keep warm."

"Yeah, heh, heh, heh. You, too. Heh, heh, heh. Boogadee, boogadee, the monsters are coming to get you. Gonna eat you for lunch." He wiped his brow again, grinning like a lunatic. "Come through the snow and bite your heads off." He laughed so hard, Joey was afraid he would have a stroke.

"Catch you later," Joey said, getting up to leave.

THE DEAD OF WINTER

"Not if the monsters get you first," Charlie said. He drained his glass and refilled it from the bottle Joey had brought him. Getting hammered was one way to ride out the storm, Joey thought. Maybe not the worst.

15

Joey topped off the Arctic Cat's gas tank from his jerry can before they headed back toward town. As cold and miserable as it was outside, it was a relief to be free of the stench in Charlie's house. Out here, the air was fresh, if bracing.

"He knows more than he's saying," Frank said, his voice muffled by the scarf wrapped around his face.

Joey stopped pouring. "What makes you say that?"

"He's scared of something. Terrified."

"Your Spidey senses tingling?"

"Laugh all you want, buddy, but I know when someone's lying or deflecting. I've had plenty of practice," he said. "Growing up with you, I mean."

Joey grabbed a handful of snow and whipped it at his brother. It was powdery, so the projectile fell apart before reaching him, but he still got some on the exposed parts of Frank's face.

"Let's get out of here," Frank said, wiping his cheek with a gloved hand. "I'm freezing."

When he reached Willow Avenue, Joey pulled into the grocery store parking lot. The only vehicle around was a black Polaris snowmobile parked near the main entrance. The building was dark. The front door hung askew, as if it had been forced open. He pointed it out to his brother, who nodded. Joey parked next to the Polaris and cut the engine.

"Might not be a good idea to go in if the bad guys are still here," Frank said. "Worse if they're armed."

"I'm pretty sure that's Bob Haber's machine. He owns the store."

Still, they approached the entrance with caution and squeezed through the damaged door. A small snowdrift had formed in the entryway, and they saw footprints leading both in and out.

"Bob?" Joey called out. "You here?"

"Hope you're not coming to rob me, too," a man's voice said.

"It's Joey Shaw," he said. "I've got my brother with me."

They stepped farther inside the store. Almost no light penetrated the full-height glass windows along one wall due to the snow piled against them and the overcast conditions outside. Joey was reminded of a movie he'd seen a few years ago where a bunch of people were trapped inside a grocery store by prehistoric monsters. That one hadn't ended well.

Out of the gloom, a man carrying a flashlight approached. "Want some steaks for dinner?" he asked. "With the power out, I won't be able to sell any of this, even if it's still good. Federal regulations. All the meat and dairy. And the frozen foods. Might as well take what you want."

"Did you call the police?"

The man, who was about fifty and looked like he hadn't shaved in three days, nodded. "Yeah, a patrol car came by a while ago. Fat lot of good it'll do. I came straight here after the power went out and found the door open. They didn't take much, but they wrecked the door. Looks like they hooked it to a winch and popped it." He surveyed the premises. "Going to have to get someone to sit guard or else they'll clean me out." He peered at Joey. "You interested?" He shook his head. "Nah, I didn't think so."

Frank stepped forward. "I think we can fix the door. And we'll pay for whatever we take."

Haber shook his head again. "I'm insured. And if you help me, you'll have my eternal gratitude as well."

It took a while, but the three men were eventually able to realign the front door to a point where the lock would engage again. "Well, that's a huge relief," Haber said. "Doesn't mean someone won't pop it again, but at least it'll keep the honest folk out."

Frank and Joey rounded up enough supplies to keep them going for several days. Frank tried to press a couple of twenties into Haber's hand, but the man refused. "You done me a favor, stopping by. I remember you—you were a good kid. I liked your parents, too." He glanced at Joey but didn't add anything to his evaluation. "Stay safe out there. Bad things can happen in a storm like this. Brings out the worst in people."

They shook hands with Haber and departed. Frank had to hold onto several bags of groceries that wouldn't fit into the Arctic Cat's storage bay, so Joey took it easy on the way home. As long as the fuel for the generator lasted, they wouldn't freeze and now they wouldn't starve, either. If nothing terrible came out of the storm, it looked like they would survive Bruno.

Joey hoped the same was true for everyone else in Bayport.

THE DEAD OF WINTER

16

After they put the groceries away and had a hearty lunch, Joey said, "What now?"

"I was thinking. Maybe we should check out the Thompson place after all. It's still empty, right?"

"Been for sale since last summer," Joey said. "Not exactly a booming real estate market around here. Why d'you want to go there?"

"Just curious, I guess."

"You want to see if there's an im-fucking-possible tunnel in the basement," Joey said.

Frank shrugged. "Why not?"

"Funny," Joey said.

"What?"

"How quick you can start thinking about crazy things as if they're perfectly normal, everyday occurrences. Is this what it's like to go insane?" He stopped. "Maybe that's it. Maybe that acid I dropped the other day was bad shit and I'm still tripping. Maybe none of this is really happening."

"Just keep telling yourself that, bro," Frank said.

"Something digging tunnels beneath a small New England town, doing away with its residents one by one. It's like a Lovecraft story."

"I think Lovecraft was more about wide scale destruction than something this close-up and personal."

"So, what? Abominable snowman? Bigfoot?" He gave Frank a look. "Chupacabra?" He stretched out the word and grinned.

Frank shrugged and picked up his parka. "Guess we'll just have to find out."

Joey paused. "Maybe we should be armed. In case we, you know, run into this killer. Man or beast or whatever?"

"So you want to go raid the gun shop now?"

"Wouldn't have to," Joey said. "I've got a few guns kicking around here."

"A few."

Joey nodded. "I like to shoot things," he said. "For fun."

"Right."

"I'm pretty good. I'm sure you are too, what with you being a cop—excuse me, a detective—and all. I saw the way you handled those zombies. Pew! Pew!"

Frank didn't say anything.

"Never know what we'll run into out there. Robbers, murderers." Joey wiggled his fingers at his brother like Charlie had. "The boogie man."

Frank was quiet for a few seconds longer. "Okay. Show me what you have."

They each picked a semi-automatic pistol from Joey's arsenal, as well as extra clips of ammo. "Is any of this even remotely legal?" Frank asked. Getting no response, he continued. "Thought not."

They geared up to go outside again and headed back to the garage. The Thompson house wasn't far away, but even a short journey would be arduous on foot.

While they cleared the snow away from in front of the garage doors—a pile had slid off the roof while they were eating—Joey said, "What if this is the way the world ends?"

"What?"

"It just keeps on snowing. Forever. No nuclear war or plague or zombie apocalypse. It snows until everything we need to survive is buried."

"Like in that Korean movie."

"Huh?"

"The one where all the survivors are on a train, going around and around the world."

"You saw that?" Joey asked.

"We get Netflix in Texas," Frank said.

"Yeah, but I didn't know that was your thing."

Frank was quiet for a moment while he dumped a load of snow at the edge of the driveway. "You know what I think?"

"That if this keeps up, we're going to run out of places to put the snow?"

Frank snorted. "I was thinking we could probably be friends if we weren't brothers." He scooped another load and pushed it into the growing pile.

Joey didn't have an answer for that.

They had to wait atop the drift at the end of the driveway for the snowplow to pass. Hector gave him a big wave on the way by. A cascade of snow from the front blade landed all around them with a resounding whoomp. Joey looked over his shoulder at the almost indiscernible bump in the snow that represented his Civic. He should have worked harder to put it in the garage the other night. He wasn't sure he'd ever see it again.

Joey guided the Arctic Cat down the middle of the street. He wouldn't have thought it possible, but the town looked more deserted than on their previous outings. Houses were all but invisible, hidden behind vast mountains of snow. He caught occasional glimpses of rooftops over the drifts. The smoke

THE DEAD OF WINTER

billowing from the chimneys was the only real indication of inhabitation. For all he knew, everyone was dead inside their homes, victims of this homicidal entity they were now tracking.

None of this made any sense to Joey. Why would it satisfy itself with one victim a month for a few months and then go dormant for nearly a year? Was it a human being or something else, something beyond their comprehension? An elder God, perhaps. Maybe Lovecraft had been onto something.

They reached the bungalow where Gerald Thompson lived until a year ago. The FOR SALE sign posted by an ambitious and optimistic realtor last June was now mostly buried in a snowdrift. Only a corner of it was visible, mangled by Hector and his wayward snowplow. No smoke billowed from this chimney, nor had anyone attempted to clear the driveway.

Joey couldn't risk taking a run at the snowbank. It was far too steep. He might have tried it if he was alone, and high, but with Frank on the back he stood a good chance of rolling over. Instead, he went down the driveway of the house next door and across the field into Thompson's backyard. It was heavy going and he almost swamped the machine a couple of times in the deep, powdery snow. After he cut the engine, he and Frank gathered their tools and waded to the back door. It wasn't quite as bad as quicksand, but it was hard going all the same.

And still the snow kept coming down. Where could it all be coming from? he wondered as Frank worked at the lock.

Joey had never been inside the house before. He'd been to the front door many times, though, either at Halloween or when canvassing for the Heart Association or the Cancer Society or whichever charity their mother was currently championing. It seemed strange to simply walk in and wander around. His flashlight beam played off sheet-covered furniture. The air smelled of dust and abandonment. The realtor or the family had essentially mothballed the place until spring. It wouldn't thaw out until June, Joey thought.

There was no point in exploring the ground floor. The basement was their destination, and they found the door leading to the cellar steps in the kitchen. Two knives had been inserted into the frame, one at the top and one near the floor. Their mother used to do the same thing whenever they went away for more than a day or two. It was to keep burglars from getting into the main house if they broke in via the basement. Joey wondered what would've happened if Mr. Thompson had sealed the basement door like this. Would he have thwarted whatever had come into his home and taken him away? Probably not, he decided, remembering the apparent violence surrounding the other holes in the concrete.

Frank pulled the knives out and placed them on the counter behind the door. "Don't let me forget to put these back when we leave," he said. It was the first time either of them had spoken since entering (*breaking* and entering, Joey reminded himself) the home of their former math teacher.

Frank led the way into the cellar, but when he reached the bottom step, he handed the flashlight to Joey. Joey wasn't sure he wanted to do this, to be confronted with yet more proof of something inexplicable, but he was here now, so he might as well go through with it.

He found what they were looking for in a section of wall next to the oil tank. Most of the walls were covered with shelves, but this section was unadorned. It also happened to have a gaping hole through it, though this one wasn't nearly as large as the other two they'd seen. *He'd* seen, rather.

"Here?" Frank asked.

"Here," Joey said. He drew an outline of the opening with his fingertip. There was a hint of that electrical smell he'd detected at the other sites, but it wasn't as strong.

"Smaller," Frank said.

Joey nodded. "I wonder what that means."

"Can you still...?"

"What?"

Frank shrugged, exaggerating the motion so it could be seen through his parka in the poor light. "Put your hand into the opening?"

Joey wasn't sure he wanted to try. The hole was plenty big, at least two feet across, but he had the sense it was closing in. He had a fleeting vision of it snapping shut on his bicep, trapping him like that mountain climber who'd been forced to cut off his arm with a penknife. He imagined something on the other side, tugging on the trapped appendage, eventually ripping it from the socket or, worse, chewing on his fingers, consuming his hand, his wrist, his forearm a bit at a time as his lifeblood oozed from the wounds and he shrieked with agony as he squirmed and struggled but couldn't possibly break free.

"Uh," he said, and looked around for a substitute for his arm. He found a push broom leaning against the wall and grabbed it. Holding it by the bottom, he shoved the handle into the hole as far as he could. He couldn't shake the notion that at any second something on the other side was going to grab the pole and pull, but if it did, better a broom handle than his arm.

"That is...so...fucking...wrong," Frank said. "It's like something from a Penn and Teller routine."

"Which one of us is which?" Joey asked

"You aren't Teller," Frank said. "You could never keep your mouth shut that long."

"Har-de-har-har-har," Joey said. He aimed the flashlight into the hole. The tunnel appeared to taper in the distance. "I think it's getting smaller," he said.

"What?"

"Like it's shrinking. Healing. If we came back in a few months, maybe it would only be this big." He touched his thumb and middle finger together to make a golf ball-sized circle.

"How's that possible?"

"How is any of this?" Joey asked. "We through here?"

"I guess," Frank said.

"What now?"

"I could use a beer. And a steak."

"Sounds good to me."

They climbed the steps to the kitchen. The instant they stepped through the door, a flashlight beam hit Joey square in the face, momentarily blinding him. "Freeze," the voice said. "Or I'll shoot."

17

Joey could tell that Chief Morton didn't appreciate it when he couldn't stop giggling at the sight of her, but bundled up in her unflattering, heavy parka with her earflaps pulled down low, she resembled that woman cop on the TV version of *Fargo*, except Morton had more freckles. And better cheekbones.

She'd holstered her service pistol when she realized who she was dealing with, but she hadn't released them, and she looked pissed, though cute at the same time, in Joey's opinion. She reminded him of his favorite weather channel reporter, he realized. "I thought we had an understanding," she said.

Frank had the good sense to look embarrassed. His head drooped like a dog's. "My investigation got complicated," he said.

"Investigation?" she said, almost shouting. "What the hell can you possibly investigate in this blizzard? Thanks to you, I had to drag my ass out of my nice warm office."

"She said 'ass,'" Joey said.

"How did you know we were here?" Frank asked, ignoring his brother's antics.

"Gertrude Hooper reported a snowmobile going through her driveway and into her neighbor's yard. Figured it was a burglar taking advantage of the storm to rob some empty houses. Someone already broke into Haber's grocery store."

Frank nodded.

"Am I correct in assuming you're on the premises without the knowledge or permission of the owner's next of kin?"

"We heard it was for sale," Joey said. "Thought we'd check it out as an investment property."

"Shut up, Joey," Frank said.

"I'm waiting for an explanation."

Frank sighed. "We have to tell her."

Joey opened his eyes wide. "What? No fucking way. She'll have us locked up."

"She can already lock us up," Frank said. "In case you didn't notice, our hands are looking pretty red."

"I'm standing right here," Morton said. "Show me *what*?"

Joey shook his head. "Uh, uh. No way."

"I can't do it without you," Frank said.

"That's right. You can't."

"Show me *what*? Don't make me break out the handcuffs."

Joey opened his mouth to make another wisecrack—anything to divert his brother from this madness—but Frank cut him off.

"Come on, Joey. We need to tell someone."

Joey let his shoulders slump. "Just don't make me do that thing with my hand."

"The broom will do," Frank said.

"You guys are weird," Morton said. "Maybe I *should* lock you up."

"Follow us," Frank said, turning back toward the basement door.

"Don't blame me if this blows your mind," Joey said. "It was his idea."

In the basement they led the police chief to the open section of wall. Frank held his flashlight to illuminate it.

Morton squinted, then shook her head. "Are you two pulling my leg?"

THE DEAD OF WINTER

Joey picked up the push broom. Morton took a step away from him and her hand drifted toward her holster.

"Chill, Chief," Joey said. "We didn't bring you down here to mug you." He paused. "But don't chill too much. This definitely isn't a chill-tastic thing I'm about to show you."

"Get on with it before I give in to the urge to shoot you."

"Okay. Okay. Don't say I didn't warn you." Holding the broom by the brush end, Joey inserted the handle into the hole. All the way. With Morton present, he was suddenly aware of how sexual it seemed, although maybe not to her.

"What the bloody fuck?" she said.

"Yeah," Joey said, pulling the broom out and leaning it against the wall. "My thoughts, exactly."

"It's some kind of a trick."

"Nope," Joey said. "Watch this. Note that at no time do my fingers ever leave my hand," he said as he repeated the demonstration with a length of 2x4 he found on the workbench. Then he chucked the wood all the way into the hole. It clattered to the ground inside. "Hear that?"

Morton shook her head back and forth slowly. Her jaw was slack.

"May I?" he asked, holding a hand out for the chief's flashlight. "Turn yours off," he told his brother. He stuck the flashlight into the hole. A second later, he withdrew it.

"What did that look like to you?" he asked his brother.

"It got dark the second it went in," he said. "The whole room."

"Not for me. I could still see the light."

"Wait...what?" Morton said. "You mean, you can't see it either?"

"Nope," Frank said. "Only Joey."

"You swear you didn't turn the flashlight off?" Morton asked.

Joey put his hand to his chest. "And hope to die."

"How on earth did you know to look here?"

"Because we found the same thing in the basement of Donna's apartment building," Frank said.

"And at Harvey Andrews' house," Joey said. Then he clapped his hand over his mouth. "We've been bad, bad boys."

Morton took the flashlight back and tapped it on the wall. It's made a solid thunk when it connected with the surface.

"The other holes were bigger. This one seems to be closing up."

"I need to sit down." Morton lowered herself onto the basement steps. "My head hurts." She looked up at the two men. "I don't know what to do with this."

Frank gave her a cock-eyed grin. "Join the club."

Morton looked at Joey. "Dare I ask what's on the other side of the wall?"

"A tunnel. This one is fairly small, but the other two are big enough to walk into. Like a mineshaft."

"That leads, where, exactly?"

Joey shrugged.

"You haven't gone in to check it out?"

"Do I look like I have a death wish?" Joey asked.

"And you're the only person who can see it."

"So far. Lucky me."

"Have you checked the houses belonging to the other people you mentioned?"

"Are you asking us to admit to additional criminal offenses?" Joey asked.

"I'm asking," and here she looked at Frank, "to be briefed on the status of your investigation."

"We haven't," he said. "I don't think we need to." He nodded at the wall. "Two vectors are enough to triangulate a location. This one just confirms it."

"What are you talking about?"

Joey spoke up. "All three shafts go in the same direction." He brought his hands forward until his fingertips touched. "I mean, they converge at a single point."

"And where's that?"

"We need to take some more accurate measurements," he said, "but somewhere near the mill pond."

Chief Morton wrinkled her nose. It was a most delightful expression, Joey thought. "What's there?"

Joey shook his head. "I have no fucking idea."

18

Before they left the Thompson house, Frank used his cell phone to get an accurate GPS location and a bearing on the direction of the tunnel. Then Frank went with Chief Morton on her official police snowmobile, a souped-up blue Yamaha Apex, to the Andrews place. Neither one would be able to see the hole, but Frank knew where it was. It made sense to have a police escort if they were going to break in somewhere. Again.

Joey returned to Donna's apartment building. The mysterious, impossible tunnel looked unchanged. Part of him

THE DEAD OF WINTER

had been hoping that it, too, would have started shrinking, because that would mean the possibility he had to go inside was shrinking, too. He knew that was what his brother would eventually decide had to be done. He hadn't come right out and said it, but it seemed inevitable.

Staring into the inky darkness, he was tempted to take the bull by the horns and walk through the portal to see where the tunnel led. He'd get the jump on Frank, surprise the fuck out of him. Maybe impress him, which was something he didn't think he'd ever done. Not even when they were kids and Joey had done one incredibly dangerous thing after another on dares from Frank and his friends. They always seemed to find some new way to torment and bedevil him, but he never complained, even when he lost a tooth or broke his arm. Did they respect him for following through on their challenges? Were they impressed? Joey very much doubted it. Mostly they laughed about it.

What he was contemplating now was as foolhardy as the swan dive off the cliff into the murky coastal waters or standing in front of a net with shabby and inadequate goalie equipment while his brother and the others took slapshots at him. If he crossed this threshold, he might never return and no one would ever know what became of him. He'd vanish like the others, as surely as if he waded into quicksand. And who would miss him? His brother, he supposed, for a while. But then Frank would go back to his busy life in Houston and immerse himself in another fascinating case, and Joey would become a distant memory. He had no legacy. There wouldn't even be a stone to show where his body rested for eternity. He would have been deleted, like text in a word processor.

CTRL-X.

Gone forever.

Of course, this fate might lie in his future anyway, but at least if it happened because Frank thought it was a good idea, his brother might feel guilty for goading him on. Guilt would be his lasting legacy, and that had a certain appeal. At least he'd be remembered.

Joey shook off the introspective moment and double checked his readings. "Measure twice, cut once," his old man used to say when they worked on projects around the house. Then he bundled up for the trip back home, where he'd compare notes with the others.

The snow hadn't eased in the least. If anything, based on the amount he had to clear off the Arctic Cat before starting the engine, it was worse than before. Was the storm connected to the disappearances? All five people had vanished during the winter. Had it been storming on each occasion? He didn't know, but if it had been...so what? It didn't seem like useful information. Just an observation. But he was no detective with a gold shield. He told himself to remember to look it up when he got back to the house. In case it was important.

Morton's Yamaha was already parked next to his house when he arrived, a fine coating of snow building up on the bench seat. He stowed the Arctic Cat in the garage and found a tarp to cover her machine. Before going inside, he topped off the generator's gas tank.

He encountered a comfortable scene, with his brother and Chief Morton sitting at the kitchen table and a pot of coffee brewing. Joey took off his boots and put them on the rubber mat behind the door. He hung his parka on a peg.

The coffee smelled wonderful. He pulled three mugs from the cabinet—all of them clean, for a wonder. Maybe he should make a habit of washing up after himself, he mused. It was sort of nice. "What do you take in yours, Chief?"

"One sugar, please," she said. "And you can call me Lauren."

"Sure thing, Chief," he said as he surveyed the room for anything incriminating. He made a pretense of wiping off the counter, then grabbed the ashtray and dumped it in the trashcan.

"Don't worry," Morton said. "I'm not going to bust you for having a couple of roaches in your ashtray."

Joey noticed the blush on his brother's face and grinned.

"Besides," she continued. "If I really wanted to bust you, I'm sure I could find plenty of other things to jam you up with." She smiled when she said this, which made Joey a little nervous. "Like breaking and entering. Or that gun tucked into your waistband, maybe?"

Joey had forgotten all about the pistol. He pulled his sweater down over it and offered his best aw-shucks grin. "You guys check out the coordinates yet?"

Frank shook his head. "We were waiting for you."

Joey wondered what they'd found to talk about before he arrived. Old times? He wouldn't have minded eavesdropping on that conversation. He poured the coffee and delivered it to the table.

Morton's walkie talkie chattered a nonstop stream of gibberish. She didn't seem to be listening, but she suddenly grabbed the radio and said, "Ten-four." Whatever

THE DEAD OF WINTER

she'd responded to, it apparently didn't require her immediate attention.

"Busy day?" Joey asked.

Morton wrinkled her nose again. "Sort of. Different problems arise when people are stuck indoors without power. More house fires. I'm waiting for a call saying someone died from carbon monoxide poisoning." She glanced at the Coleman stove.

Joey laughed. "Don't worry. I have a CO detector."

Frank looked up. "You do?"

Joey nodded. "Got it when the old man started to go batshit. Installed lots of safety gadgets back then. This place is childproof to the max." He looked around and shrugged. "Well, it used to be."

"In a day or two, cabin fever will set in," Morton continued. "We'll get more domestic violence calls. Maybe a homicide or two. People might love each other, but if they can't get away from each other for a while, pressure builds up."

"Know what you mean," Joey said. "I'm already having homicidal thoughts about him, and it's only been two days."

"Ditto," Frank said.

"You two," Morton said, taking a sip of her coffee.

"Anyone hungry?" Joey asked. "I could whip up soup and sandwiches."

"I'd kill for a sandwich," Morton said. She put a hand to her mouth and adopted a look of mock surprise. "Don't quote me on that."

After lunch, they relocated to the living room, where Joey's computer was set up. Joey sat at the keyboard and pulled up a website with interactive satellite images. First, he entered the GPS coordinates of the three "crime scenes." They corresponded with the locations of the respective houses perfectly. Then he activated an orienteering module and overlaid the first vector. He gave it an arbitrary length, sufficient to reach the Massachusetts border.

The second vector intersected the first, as expected, at a point in the swamp near the mill pond. The third vector was a bit off. "Experimental error," Frank said.

"What's there?" Morton asked.

Joey zoomed in on the satellite image until it showed only the region around where the three lines met. Even at maximum magnification, with the map starting to pixelate, they couldn't identify any distinguishing features. He made a loop with his thumb and index finger and used it to circle his nose.

Morton frowned at him.

"Fuck knows," he explained. "Fuck knows."

19

They pored over maps and performed internet searches using every possible term and phrase they could think of, but came up dry. If there was anything known about that particular section of swamp, the 'net wasn't cognizant of it.

Chief Morton—Joey still couldn't bring himself to call her Lauren, even in his head—wondered aloud if there were any old-timers in town who could tell them about the swamp.

"We thought Charlie Benson might, but we couldn't get anything out of him." Frank said.

Morton opened and closed her mouth. "You already talked to him about it?"

Joey showed her the map they'd used earlier to plot out the five victims' homes. "It was a working theory," he said. "We have much better information now."

"If we checked out the other places," she asked, "would that help narrow it down?"

Frank shook his head. "Even if we had the spot pinpointed to the square inch, can you imagine what it's like out there right now? Would you risk your life crossing the terrain in this?" He gestured toward the living room window, outside of which the snow was blowing sideways. The wind howled and the house creaked in response.

Morton shook her head.

"Damn straight," Joey said. "We'd probably land in a deep pit of water. A bottomless pit."

"So, what, then? Do we just give up?"

"If we do, someone else will vanish," Frank said. "Soon."

"Assuming your theory is correct," Morton said.

Frank nodded.

Joey leaned back in his chair and waited for the inevitable decision. Frank seemed unwilling to meet his gaze.

"What?" Morton said.

"There's only one way to attack this problem that doesn't have the three of us wandering around in the middle of the swamp in this blizzard," Joey said.

"And that is...?"

"I have to go into one of the tunnels. By myself, since I seem to be the only person on the planet who can see them."

"But that's—"

"Crazy? Insane?" Joey said. "Tell me about it. I'm certainly open to any other suggestions."

The room fell silent except for the sound of the forced air coming through the registers and the wind whipping around the corner of the house.

Eventually, Morton spoke up. "No one can force you to do this."

"No, but they can guilt me into it." He looked at his brother as he said this. Then he looked at the chief. "Anyway. Donna was my friend, too. I need to find out what happened to her if I can."

"Where do we go in?" Frank asked.

"Again with the 'we,'" Joey said with a smirk. "I figure *we'll* draw less of an audience if *we* go in via Harvey Andrews' basement. Some of Donna's neighbors might wonder why *we're* messing around in her apartment building."

"Makes sense. What supplies do we need?" Morton asked.

"Rope," Frank said.

"What for?" Joey asked.

"So we can pull your scrawny ass out if something goes wrong."

"I see two flaws with that."

Frank asked his question without saying a word.

Joey raised his index finger. "One, I don't think anything will happen if either of you tugs on this hypothetical safety rope. From your perspective, it will probably look like it's stuck in a cement wall."

"Granted. And...?"

"Do you have any idea how much four miles of rope weighs?"

Frank opened and closed his mouth. "Oh," he said.

"Right. So, what I need is this: water, some food, a flashlight with extra batteries, a two-way radio—though I have my doubts it'll work underground—and..." He paused and looked at Morton. "...an automatic pistol with a shitload of ammunition. I want to be able to take down Bigfoot, if that's what I run into. And his whole family, if necessary. All the Bigfeet."

"Aren't you forgetting something?" Morton asked.

"Probably. Like my common sense and better judgment. What are you thinking of?"

"It's traditional to take a vial of holy water, isn't it?" She grinned at him, though it seemed forced. She's worried about me, he thought. That's interesting.

"Sure. I'll try anything. Give me a cross, too, while you're at it. I'll go all Kolchak on its ass."

Her brow furrowed.

"*The Night Stalker?* Darren McGavin? No? Honey, when I get back from this fool's errand, I'm going to have to educate you in the classics."

She blushed. She actually blushed, Joey realized. And I called her "honey," he thought. Somedays pigs actually fly.

"I'll get the gun and ammo from the armory at HQ," she said, regaining her usual cool demeanor. "And the radio. Be back soon. Don't do anything without me."

"Don't worry," Joey said. "I'm in no hurry to leap into the abyss. Staring into it's bad enough."

After she left, the brothers rounded up the other items Joey needed. He found an old burlap backpack to put everything in. He also refreshed the batteries in the flashlight they'd been using all day.

"One more thing," he said before they put on their outerwear. He rummaged around in a drawer in the living room and came up with a plastic bag stuffed with grass and some rolling papers. Before his brother could voice any objections, Joey said, "If you think I'm going in there straight, you've got another think coming. I'd get drunk, too, if we had time."

He rolled two tight joints and returned the gear to the drawer. He dug out a lighter and lit one after dampening the paper by sticking the joint in his mouth for a second. After he inhaled deeply, he handed the joint over to his brother. Frank hesitated, but then relented and took a puff. "Good for you," Joey said as he expelled a lungful of smoke. "High times, here we come."

They shared the joint until they got a call from Chief Morton saying she was on her way to the Andrews house and would meet them there.

"Shhhh." Frank said, putting his hand over the receiver when Joey started giggling. "Gotta go," he told Morton. "See you there." He disconnected the call and went into the kitchen. "You're going to need more food," he said. "Definitely."

20

Chief Morton tried to look disapproving when she met up with the brothers behind Harvey Andrews' abandoned house, but she couldn't pull it off. "I thought I told you not to do anything without me," she said.

"Do you want a hit?" Joey asked. "Because that could be arranged." He was transfixed by her crystalline green eyes and the way her freckles seemed to dance around on her cheeks.

"You're offering illegal substances to the chief of police?" She stared at him but he didn't look away.

"Another time, perhaps?" Joey said, wiggling his eyebrows. "When you're not in uniform."

Being high did nothing to minimize the effects of the cold, blustery weather, so it felt good to be inside, even with the heat turned off. Joey stripped off his bulky parka and heavy boots. He pulled a hooded windbreaker over the shirts he was wearing, and donned a comfortable pair of sneakers. In the unlikely event he got too warm in the tunnel, he could remove layers as he went.

Morton had brought a compact and intense flashlight with two extra sets of batteries. He checked out the gun, a pitch black Glock 41 with a thirteen bullet clip, making sure he understood how to operate it, and tucked the extra clips into the windbreaker's pockets where he could get at them quickly if needed. Then he tested the two-way radio and attached it to his belt.

"All right," he said, squaring his shoulders. "Let's do this."

They descended the basement stairs single file. On the way, Frank grabbed a box of Honeycomb cereal from the overhead pantry shelf. Morton, who was between Frank and Joey, poked the older brother in the shoulder.

"What?" he said. "We might get hungry waiting for him to get back."

She scoffed at him and poked again. "Get going."

At the bottom of the steps, Frank turned on the battery-powered fluorescent Coleman lantern he'd remembered to bring at the last second. When he held it high and led the way past the workbench and the door to the backyard, Joey was reminded of drawings of Diogenes, who carried a lantern in broad daylight, in search of an honest man.

Frank stopped after he rounded the corner behind the furnace. "Still there, right?" he asked.

"Large as life," Joey said. "Unfortunately for me."

Morton dug into her pants pocket and came up with a piece of chalk, which she handed to Joey. "Show us exactly where it is," she said.

Holding the chalk sideways, Joey outlined the perimeter of the hole.

"That big," she said, her voice filled with awe.

Joey stuck the chalk into his pocket and nodded. "Be right back," he said. As he headed toward the laundry room, he heard Morton say, "What's he up to?"

"Who knows?" his brother responded. "Probably went to take a last-minute leak."

Joey grinned as he grabbed four enormous packages of toilet paper, each holding thirty-six triple-ply rolls. He juggled the stack as he groped his way to the rear of the basement again.

"You trying to tell us something?" Morton asked.

"Better than sitting on the basement floor," Joey said. He made two stacks against the wall. "I'm going to be a while. Thought you should be comfortable while you wait."

Frank hung the lantern from a hook in the ceiling and put the box of cereal on the floor between them. "Looks like we're all set," he said.

Joey figured he'd delayed the inevitable long enough. He rechecked his gear, reconfirmed the two-way connection with Morton's handset, stuck the Glock in his waistband after giving it a final going over, and took a deep breath.

"Here goes nothing," he said, taking a step toward the hole in the wall. His brother approached and they had an awkward moment staring at each other until they finally tacitly agreed that a handshake was in order.

"Wonder if I should've made out a will," Joey said. He noticed Chief Morton standing behind Frank and decided she deserved a handshake, too. They were all in this together, after all. He stuck his hand out, but she shook her head.

"No way, buddy boy," she said. As he lowered his hand, somewhat hurt, she stepped forward, put her hands on his shoulders, looked him square in the eyes and kissed him. On the lips. It was moist but relatively chaste, and if he hadn't been battling the conflicting emotions of terror and despair, compounded by being high and a tad paranoid, he might've made more of it. "Shit," he said. "Wow. Now I gotta come back," he said.

"You better," Morton said.

THE DEAD OF WINTER

Joey saw a glint in her eyes and realized she was as frightened as he was. Well, maybe not quite, he thought. Her neck wasn't on the line.

With that, he turned and put his right foot through the hole. The lower edge was only a few inches off the ground. His leg tingled as it passed through the invisible threshold. It wasn't an unpleasant sensation.

"I can't look," he heard Chief Morton say behind him. He planted his leading foot on the ground and shifted his weight, pulling the rest of his body through. The tingling sensation traversed his body. It was sort of erotic, he thought, but that might have been the weed talking. It also felt at least twenty degrees colder than in the basement.

He turned to look at his brother and the police chief. He waved, but they just stared blankly at him. They can't see me, he reminded himself. He could strip naked and dance the watusi—whatever the hell that was—and they'd never know. He giggled, imagining the reaction he'd get if his dick flopped through the hole in the wall. How it would look from their perspective.

"Time to get serious," he said. Before setting out, he unclipped the two-way radio and pressed the button. "Testing...testing..."

The duo on the other side of the semipermeable barrier didn't react.

"Testing," he repeated. "Frank Shaw is a big, fat ninny," he said.

Nothing.

"Police Chief Morton has amazing tits."

Still nothing.

He pulled his cell phone from his pants pocket. *No Signal*, the display proclaimed. He sighed. He really was going to have to do this alone. He put the phone away, then leaned through the hole into the basement, holding out the two-way radio.

"Guess I won't be needing—"

"Holy Mary, mother of God," Chief Morton said, her face as white as snow. "That is the freakiest fucking thing I have ever seen." She marched over and grabbed the radio from Joey. "Don't you ever do anything like that again or I'll kick your ass, motherfucker."

She was shaking. Joey grinned at his brother. "She's got a mouth, doesn't she? I like it."

Frank, who was probably still as high as Joey was, put his hands over his eyes. "You look like one of those Nazis stuck in the walls of the castle in that movie *The Keep*."

"Awesome," Joey said. He extended his arms and leaned back and forth. The tingling sensation and the change in temperature told him each time he crossed the threshold.

"Shit," Morton said. "You remind me of Han Solo emerging from the carbonite."

"A young Harrison Ford," Joey said. "I'll take that." He winked at her. "Though I feel more like Indiana Jones at the moment. I hope I don't encounter a big boulder down there. Anyway, as I was saying, the walkie doesn't work. Cell phone either. Thought you should know." He gave a mock salute. "Well, I'm off again. To-doo-lee-oo," he said.

"Wait," Frank said. "We won't be able to contact you."

Joey leaned through the wall again. Morton flinched. "Sorry, sorry." He turned to his brother. "I can hear you fine. If you want to say something to me, just yell." He glanced at Morton. "And remember I can see you, so don't do anything you wouldn't want me to see."

She stuck her tongue out at him. It was a lovely tongue.

This farewell party was taking too long, so he decided to end it. "Catch you on the flipside," he said and turned back into the tunnel.

He panned the light Morton had given him around the walls. They were rough and uneven. The floor was clear of debris. He wondered again what could possibly create such a monumental excavation. It was almost as if something had eaten its way through the rock and earth. His chemically altered brain conjured up images of enormous earthworms, like the ones in a book he'd read a few years ago, or the sandworms in *Dune*. At least the walls of the tunnel weren't slimy, so it probably wasn't conqueror worms. He pretended to straighten a non-existent Stetson. "Snakes," he said. "Why did it have to be snakes?" He took a step forward. Could be mutant moles, he thought. Or big rats with huge fangs and long naked tales.

None of this was improving his spirits in the least. He turned for one last glance at the world he was leaving behind, wondering if he'd ever see his brother again. Or Chief Morton, who had so surprised him with a memorable kiss. That deserved further exploration, he decided.

Nothing for it then. He had to come back.

THE DEAD OF WINTER

21

Aliens, he thought as he advanced down the dark corridor. Maybe we're dealing with alien abductions, like on *The X-Files*. But why would they go to all the trouble of making tunnels when they could teleport people into their flying saucers?

Maybe smoking that joint hadn't been such a good idea after all. Now he couldn't rid his mind of the image of those grey aliens with the big heads and oversized bottomless eyes. Or, worse, the other alien, the one that had burst through that guy's chest and almost sent Joey into a conniption fit. He'd been high the first time he'd seen that and had screamed.

He double-checked the pistol in his waistband and decided he felt better holding it in his hand. He didn't want it getting tangled up in his clothes if he needed it. He only hoped whatever he encountered down here was vulnerable to human technology. That it wasn't some superhuman entity that would laugh in its creepy, otherworldly voice as bullets bounced off its carapace before it plucked the gun from Joey's hand and then grabbed him around the waist and stuffed his body into its gaping maw.

That would suck.

The tunnel had been as straight as an arrow so far, which had been their fundamental assumption, but what if it started to curve? Would he notice? Or, worse, what if it branched? He started humming, though he couldn't identify the song. Probably something he'd listened to while high. He regretted not bringing his iPod along—this could be a long trek. It was roughly four miles to the spot where the vectors intersected, which meant at least an hour on foot. He should have brought a bicycle—that would have sped the process up. He had too much time on his hands to think, that was the problem. He was nobody's hero, but he was eager to get to the other end of the passage and confront whatever he'd find there. This slow-motion sneak attack wasn't for him.

If he extended his arms, he could almost touch the walls. As he marched along, constantly focused on the point where the light faded to darkness, he was tempted to shut the flashlight off. See if he could maintain a straight line. The light was both a blessing and a curse. He'd see something in the distance, but it would see him, too. On the other hand, if it was some kind of a mole creature, light would be an advantage. A weapon, even, if the creature wasn't used to the light.

Creatures, creatures, creatures, he chided himself. Whatever had he gotten himself into, agreeing to do this? And why him? What was so special about him? Nothing, according to most of the people in his life. Nothing whatsoever.

Movement at the outer edge of the flashlight beam caught his attention. He stopped, pulse racing, and slowly turned to his left. A design was dancing on the tunnel wall, like something out of a kaleidoscope, all reds and oranges and yellows. He looked at it, fascinated. It was like staring into flames.

In fact, it was exactly like staring into flames, although closer than he'd ever been before. The marijuana high made him endlessly fascinated. He eased forward and extended a hand, expecting to detect warmth, but this section of wall felt no different than its surroundings. He took a half step back. The dancing colors were surrounded by a rectangular block with rounded corners. Was this some kind of message from the entity that had created this tunnel?

He thought some more about where he was headed, then slapped his forehead. The tunnel was a straight line from Harvey Andrews' basement to the swamp. It started off seven or eight feet below the ground and, as far as Joey could tell, it didn't seem to be descending. That meant the tunnel passed through the basements of any number of houses along the way. Businesses, too, and who knew what else? At the moment, it was intersecting someone's furnace. Joey had no idea how such a thing could be true, how it and the furnace could coexist without one affecting the other, but then again, none of this made any sense. Not only were the flames not hot—he supposed the tunnel created a force field to hold them in place—but presumably the rest of the furnace, where he was standing, still existed to an outside observer. If someone looked into the combustion chamber, they probably wouldn't see him lurking among the flames like Shadrach, Meshach, and Abednego, names he summoned from a long-ago Sunday School class.

He continued on, checking the wall from time to time. Since the power was out in town, people probably weren't making much use of their basements, which was good because he thought there was a chance the tunnel would transect a person who stood in the right—or wrong—place as he was passing by, and that was a sight he wasn't ready to face, especially not in his current condition.

THE DEAD OF WINTER

At one point, he encountered an oval inscribed in the wall that was probably a water pipe, cut on a bias, or a sewer line. No way he was going anywhere near that, but at least there was no smell. In fact, it had been a while since he'd detected anything other than his own perspiration.

It was deathly quiet in here, too. Only the sounds of his feet on the ground and his backpack contents jiggling on his shoulder interrupted the preternatural silence. It was like he was passing through another dimension or reality. Maybe that was it—maybe he was traveling down some kind of wormhole. Just not the kind made by an actual worm. A highway to hell, to borrow a phrase. Like Morton had said—a Twilight Zone. Was he traveling farther and farther away from his own reality, soon to emerge in some bizarre, Lovecraftian world where none of the ordinary rules applied, or was he on a parallel, skimming past the "real world"? Deep thoughts, he told himself. Plenty of questions; no answers.

He carried on. The health app on his smartphone told him he'd been underway for nearly thirty minutes, and had covered almost two miles. About halfway there, wherever *there* was. Then what?

He fell into a kind of waking trance, one foot in front of the other, the flashlight beam aimed forever into the distance. He hummed to himself to break the monotony and keep his wits sharp, but the only songs that came to mind were dire. "Don't Fear the Reaper." "The Eve of Destruction." "Everything's Ruined." "I See a Darkness." They didn't exactly buoy his spirits.

Something white flashed in his beam. He spun around and came face-to-face with a grinning skull. He gasped and stepped back, almost losing hold of his flashlight and pistol. His thoughts raced—was this Harvey Andrews? Or Donna?

He took a deep breath to get himself under control. He panned the light along the tunnel wall and saw more bones and skeletons. A lot of them. As far as the eye could see, and on both sides. They were all pointed in the same direction, fairly evenly spaced. All were lying on their backs.

Though rattled, he did the math. The graveyard. He was passing through the St Catherine's Catholic Church Cemetery, which was along the vector between the Andrews place and the swamp. Unnerved by the long line of dead men, women and children, he kept his gaze fixed on the distance and didn't allow himself to look left or right. This went on for some time; the graveyard was sizable, with plots that dated back to colonial days.

One step in front of another. Eyes on the prize. Nothing to see here, folks. Just keep walking.

After several minutes, he allowed himself a glance at the wall to his right. All clear. He'd passed through the underworld and come out on the other side.

Shaken by the experience, he took a few deep breaths and tried to get his head back in the game. The dope was wearing off, which was either a good thing or bad, depending on how he looked at it. Did he really want to be straight when he confronted whatever lay ahead?

One foot in front of the other.

The flashlight was getting noticeably dimmer, so he stopped long enough to install fresh batteries. The last thing he needed was to get wherever the hell he was headed and suddenly find himself in the dark. He also had a few swigs of water and a handful of chips. "Snack of champions," he muttered before setting off again.

He was starting to think they had made a calculation error and underestimated where his destination was supposed to be when he noticed a subtle change in the tunnel. Up ahead it looked as if it was getting wider. Much wider. A cave, he decided.

He shrugged off the backpack, leaving it on the floor so as to be unencumbered, checking his pockets to make sure he had the extra magazines and tightening his grip on the pistol.

There didn't seem much point in approaching slowly since the flashlight beam had already announced his presence, so he sped up, hoping to take advantage of the element of surprise.

This is it, he told himself as he rushed to the end of the tunnel into the chamber ahead.

22

He burst into the expansive room and crouched, swinging the pistol and flashlight in tandem the way he'd seen cops do it on TV. He almost shouted "clear" once he was sure there was nothing dangerous around and decided maybe the pot hadn't yet worn off completely after all.

THE DEAD OF WINTER

Joey took a few moments to evaluate his surroundings. He was in a domed cavern, like salt domes he'd read about where they collected methane. Places that occasionally exploded, causing artificial earthquakes. They had those in Texas, where his brother now lived.

He sniffed the air. No gas, just that unusual electrical odor he'd detected at the tunnel entrance. The chamber was easily twenty feet across, and more or less round. The roof was at least ten feet over his head, if not more. That meant it might extend above the surface of the swamp, assuming the tunnel hadn't led him deeper into the earth, which was possible, he supposed. He fished his cell phone out of his pocket. No signal, of course, so he couldn't get a GPS reading. Though there was no way to determine exactly where he was, he had no reason to doubt their calculations.

He captured video of the room so he could describe it to the others later. The tunnel that had brought him here was one of three. The entrances to the others were fairly close to the one he'd emerged from. There were also three smaller holes, like the one they'd found in Gerald Thompson's cellar. "Healing tunnels" was how Joey thought of them.

Three tunnels, three former tunnels. He could account for five of them, but where did the sixth one lead? He had a pretty good idea, and if he was right it explained some things, in a fucked up, twisted kind of way.

Equally as disturbing was his discovery of a shaft in the middle of the floor. He had narrowly avoided falling into it when he charged into the cave, more by luck than design. It was about four feet in diameter and seemed to lead straight down. Struck by inspiration, he used the piece of chalk Lauren had given him to outline it for the camera. He had no idea if anything would show up for the others. This whole cavern might be nothing more than a black spot to them, but it was worth a try.

He was sure that at any moment something would erupt from the shaft. His active and somewhat altered mind, still in the grips of mild paranoia, supplied a steady stream of possibilities, from the enormous snake he'd imagined before, to a horde of rats and spiders, to a great gush of black goop that would encompass his body, digesting him from the outside in as it pulled him inexorably toward the hole and down into the deep, dark earth. He even had a brief mental image of a cartoonish devil, fluorescent red with horns, a villain's mustache and a pointed tail, arriving on a sulfurous cloud and carrying a pitchfork to claim his soul.

He clung to the flashlight like a lifeline as he planted his feet solidly near the edge of the opening and leaned over a few degrees to peer into the pit. The gun felt a bit foolish—of what use would it be against any of the things he'd imagined? But it gave him some small measure of comfort, so he kept it in his hand.

Breathing shallowly through his open mouth, he knelt to get a closer look. The flashlight beam barely penetrated the darkness, revealing only the first few feet of the pit. For all he knew, that's all there was. However, there was no way in hell he was going to stick his hand in there to find out. He'd seen enough horror movies to know how that usually ended.

He looked around for something to throw into the pit, but the floor of the chamber was pristine. He took one of the magazines from his coat pocket and pried out a .45 caliber bullet. He looked at it for several seconds, admiring the way the brass shell reflected the flashlight beam. He remembered a scene from a TV show where the hero, one badass motherfucker, had thrown a bullet at his nemesis after knocking him to the floor. Joey nodded to himself and tossed the bullet over the edge, repeating the hero's perfect line. "Next one's coming faster."

He counted to himself, one one-thousand, two one-thousand, getting all the way to ten before deciding that even if the bullet struck something now, he wouldn't likely hear it. He held his breath and leaned forward, tilting his head to one side and straining for the slightest of noises.

His overactive imagination supplied a monster, like the one that guy found in a crate under the stairs at the university in *Creepshow*, lying in wait a few feet below the surface. There'd been no noise from the bullet because it had fallen into the monster's gaping maw. Now it was waiting for Joey to lean a bit farther to leap out and sink its saber-like fangs into his neck and pull him into its hidey-hole.

He straightened up and backed away from the shaft. Then he imagined something emerging from one of the tunnel openings behind him, a big lumbering beast like Poe's orangutan, swinging a huge club down onto the back of his head while he was preoccupied.

I've really got to quit doing drugs, he thought. *Or watching horror movies. One or the other. Maybe both.*

THE DEAD OF WINTER

There wasn't much more he could accomplish here, he decided, and the longer he stayed, the greater the risk he'd encounter something he could go the rest of his life without seeing. There was no trace of Donna or any of the other missing people, so what point was there in hanging around? Besides, he told himself, his brother and the chief would probably be worried about him. Unless, he thought, they'd decided to rekindle their old relationship and were now shagging each other silly while he was out here risking his life. That's what would happen in a horror movie. He imagined them getting tangled up in all that toilet paper he'd brought out for their comfort before pushing that image away. He couldn't afford to be distracted by imaginary jealousy.

He took one more pass around the cavern to make sure he hadn't overlooked anything. The wall opposite the tunnel entrances was smooth and solid. The bulk of the swamp was off in that direction. No homes for potential victims.

Giving the bottomless shaft a wide berth, he returned to face the tunnel entrances. The one he'd emerged from was to the left. He could see his backpack on the ground half a dozen feet beyond the entrance. There were small "healing tunnels" on either side of it. One would lead to Gerald Thompson's basement and the other most likely went to Eddie Jamieson's place, if he had his geography straight. Then there were two adjacent tunnel openings and a final healing tunnel that would open into Mrs. McCarthy's basement.

Of the two other tunnels, one lead to Donna's apartment building. The one on the right he decided. He supposed he could explore it, but what would that gain him? He could circle around and sneak up on Chief Morton and his brother from behind, give them the fright of their lives, but he wasn't dressed for the outdoors. Not in this weather.

He aimed the flashlight beam down the remaining tunnel, confident he knew where it went. This one *felt* newer than the others, as if it was still forming, though he couldn't explain why. He had an idea that if he started down it, he would reach a point where it ended abruptly. But for how long? And was it forming itself, or was some creature, some arcane miner, in there right this minute, laboring away like a Lovecraftian dwarf, digging, digging, digging with single-minded intent, focused on reaching its next victim?

And what would happen if it decided to take a break and head back to its subterranean lair for a spot of dinner, punching out the time clock like those cartoon dogs, so its companion could take the next shift.

Joey decided it would be a good idea to be somewhere else if that happened. He figured he had a rendezvous with this… whatever it was…in the not-too-distant future, but not now. Not here, where there was no one to hear him scream.

He dashed back into the tunnel, pausing only long enough to pick up and shoulder his backpack. As much as he wanted to—as much as his mind screamed at him that he needed to—he never once looked behind him. That was when the monsters got you, he knew. One foot in front of the other and never look back.

23

The trip back to Harvey Andrews' basement seemed to take less time than the outbound journey, but return trips usually do, Joey thought. Part of it probably had to do with the fact he wasn't high anymore—a situation he briefly considered rectifying—but much of it was because he was heading towards relative safety instead of plunging blindly toward the unknown.

He didn't even feel the need to pretend to ignore the rows of skeletal remains when he passed through the cemetery, but he'd never look at the place the same way again and made a mental note to make sure to specify cremation in the will he planned to write as soon as possible.

As he approached the far entrance to the tunnel—or, as he preferred to think of it, the exit—drawn like a moth to the Coleman lantern Frank had hung from the rafter, he was tempted to break into a run and leap into the basement to give his brother a good fright. If Chief Morton hadn't been there, he might have, despite the strong probability he'd smash into the wall and injure himself.

When he got to the shimmering window that generated that annoying burnt odor, he stopped. His two champions were seated side-by-side on the stacks of toilet paper, intent on their mobile phones. The box of cereal was open on the floor between them. His first inclination was to be hurt by their apparent lack of concern over his well-being, but he reconsidered after a second's reflection. He'd been gone for over two hours—how attentive could they remain, staring at a blank wall for all that time?

He searched his pockets, but all he found were the spare magazines for the pistol Morton had lent him. He pried another bullet from the top of a clip and lobbed it onto the floor in front of Morton and his brother. They both immediately stopped what they were doing and looked up.

Joey stepped slowly through the portal into the basement, feeling like a man returning from an interstellar mission.

Chief Morton knelt and picked up the bullet. "Hey, buddy. That's town property," she said before approaching him and pulling him into a close embrace.

Caught off guard, Joey held his hands out straight behind her, unsure what to do with them. Then he returned the hug and felt her squeeze him even tighter. His body started to respond in a way that could ruin the moment, so he released her and took a step back. He pointed at the bullet in her hand. "I hope you don't have to account for all of those, because I had to leave one behind."

"You shoot someone?" Frank asked. "Or something?"

"No. I'll tell you all about it," Joey said, "but let's go home first. I'm famished."

24

It was fully dark when they stepped out the back door of Harvey Andrews' house. At least another ten inches of snow had accumulated. The two snowmobiles were amorphous blobs. After they cleaned them off, Joey had a hard time getting his started, but it finally fired up.

Chief Morton led the way. Joey was tempted to try to pass her, turn it into a race, but her machine was sleeker and faster, and he had the extra weight of his brother on the back. Besides, he told himself, maybe it was time to start acting more like a 30-year-old instead of the overgrown kid he'd been pretending to be for years.

When they got to the house, they spent some time clearing away the snow in front of the garage doors so they could get both machines inside, out of the storm. Joey checked the generator while the other two went in to start making something to eat.

He looked up at the sky, where a three-quarter moon was only faintly visible through the cloud cover. The falling flakes were large and fluffy. He could feel the impact of each one that alighted on his cheeks. They came down in a steady stream, as if the clouds contained an endless supply of them and they wouldn't stop falling until everything on earth was buried.

Frank had turned up the thermostat, so warm air was flowing into the kitchen. When he'd purchased the gas-powered generator, their father had also installed a fuel tank in the garage, so they were in good shape for a while yet. Joey wondered how everyone else in Bayport was faring. There were probably some chilly houses in the neighborhood this night.

Chief Morton—after that embrace, maybe he should start calling her Lauren—was rummaging through the spice cabinets. Most of its contents dated back to when their mother was still alive. Joey wasn't exactly sophisticated around the kitchen. Lauren removed the caps from a few bottles and sniffed the contents. She shook her head but didn't return them to the cabinet, so apparently she deemed them acceptable. She made some sort of concoction she used to coat the three steaks Frank had laid out from the refrigerator, part of the supplies they'd picked up earlier at the grocery store.

She put a large frying pan on the Coleman stove and lit the flame. Once it was hot, Lauren put on the steaks and pushed them around until they were all flat on the surface of the pan. While they sizzled, she put together a tossed salad.

Joey hardly ever brought any of his girlfriends back here because the place was a dump most of the time. He could get used to this, he thought. Having a woman around the house. This woman in particular. How had Frank described her as a teenager? Hell on wheels and live as a firecracker. Now she was a pistol-packing mama, he thought, then grinned.

Soon the kitchen was filled with the savory aroma of the spice-coated steaks. Lauren flipped them over after a couple of minutes. "Medium rare?" she asked.

Frank nodded.

"Medium for me," Joey said, which earned him a withering glare from the self-appointed chef.

"What?" Lauren asked, catching the look on his face.

"Nothing," Joey said. "I'll have it however you want."

That seemed to satisfy her. "Don't suppose you have any wine."

"Sorry. Just beer."

THE DEAD OF WINTER

"That'll have to do. You two get the table ready," she said. "These will be ready in a few minutes."

While they ate, Joey reported on his adventures in the tunnel and the cavern beyond. He described everything in as much detail as possible, but held back the part about the cemetery. That could wait until they were done eating, at least.

The steaks were pink in the middle—almost red—but Joey had to admit they were delicious. "This might well be the best steak I've ever eaten," he told Lauren, waiting for an "I told you so" that never came. Instead she only smiled. It lit up her face.

"So there was no sign of Donna or the others?" Frank asked.

Joey shook his head as he finished chewing on a piece of steak. "Who knows what was down that shaft?" He shrugged. As he expected, neither his brother nor Lauren were able to see anything on the videos or photos he'd taken inside the cave. "I figured it was a one-way journey to the center of the earth if I tried. There's nothing to tie a rope to, even if I'd brought any with me, and I didn't feel up to a chimney climb."

He waited until they were finished to draw a diagram of the six tunnels he'd seen. From left to right, the pattern was small-big-small-big-big-small. "This is the one I came out of," he said, writing an A in the circle for Harvey Andrews.

He put T, J and M over the smaller tunnels for Thompson, Jamieson and McCarthy. Then he put a D in the big circle farthest to the right. "This one goes to Donna's apartment building."

"And this one?" Lauren asked, tapping a neatly manicured index finger on the large circle in the middle. Joey had never noticed her fingers before.

"That one," he said, pausing for a swig of beer. "I'm pretty sure that one leads to our basement."

"But we've already checked the basement," Frank protested.

Joey nodded. "I know. I got the feeling this tunnel is incomplete."

"So you think you're next," Lauren said.

The sound of Frank's fingernail scraping against his beer bottle label filled the silence.

"I think that's why I can see the tunnels," Joey said a moment later.

"Do you think this...whatever it is...is after you because you can see evidence of its existence, or can you see the signs because it's after you?" Lauren stopped, leaving her mouth open for a second. "I can't believe I just uttered that sentence."

"Crazy, right? And to answer your question…" He repeated the gesture with his fingers around his nose.

She expelled a lungful of air. "So what do we do? How do we defend against something when we have no idea what it is?"

"Arm ourselves to the teeth," Frank said. "Shotguns, machetes—"

Joey interrupted him. "Flamethrowers, acid." He smirked. "Crosses, holy water, suits of armor."

"I'm serious," Lauren said.

"Me, too, kinda. We have to cover all the bases. What if it turns out to be a pool of black goop, like that stuff that got Tasha Yar on *Star Trek*?"

"Sentient goop," Frank said, nodding. "Or a cloud of smoke like on *Lost*."

"You two," Lauren said. "We have to take this seriously."

"Oh, I am, believe you me," Joey said. "Serious as if my life depended upon it—oh, wait! It does."

"A flamethrower?"

Joey smirked. "I'm sure we can cobble something together. Fire, water, bullets, religious icons, bullets, blades. What else?"

"You said bullets twice. It would be a whole lot easier if we had some idea of what we were up against," Lauren said. She looked at Frank. "You're being awfully quiet."

"I was thinking," he said, "About something Charlie Benson said."

"Charlie?" Lana said. "What does he have to do with any of this?"

"Proximity," Frank said. "He lives on the edge of the swamp. Not far from the point of intersection on our map. Always has, as far as I know. I wonder why."

Joey asked, "What did he say that has you so interested in him. We didn't get anything useful out of him earlier."

"Remember, as we were leaving, he said something about the monster coming out of the snow to bite our heads off?"

"Bogadee, bogadee," Joey said, waving his hands like he was casting a spell.

"He said it a couple of times. I'm pretty sure he knows more than he's saying. Have all of the disappearances happened during snowstorms?"

Joey paused. "I was thinking about that earlier. I meant to bring it up," he said. "Not as bad as this one, but yeah."

"We need to visit him again."

THE DEAD OF WINTER

Lauren wrinkled her nose. "That place is gross."

"We'll go first thing in the morning," Joey said. "Really early. Catch him while he's hung over and hasn't had his hair of the dog."

"Or cat," Lauren said. "Seriously, that place is a dump. The town should've condemned it a long time ago."

Her radio crackled and she fielded a call from one of her officers. So far this evening, the town had been fairly quiet, in part because the main phone lines were down now, too, in addition to the electricity. Cell towers were failing, either because of the snow or because battery backups were running out.

While she handled the latest crisis, Joey gathered the dishes from the table and took them to the kitchen sink. He picked up the flashlight he'd used in the tunnel and descended the basement stairs. In the near darkness, he took a few seconds to get his bearings. His sense of direction was fairly reliable, though. He put a finger in the air as if testing for the wind. "That way," he muttered, pointing at the northeast corner. It was where they used to store vegetables during the winter, although no one had done that for many years. He shone the intense beam on the wall, which looked solid. And yet...

He ran his hand over the rough surface and withdrew it immediately. He felt that same, strange tingling sensation he'd experienced when passing through the opening into the tunnel. He closed his eyes and inhaled. There it was, faint but detectable. That odor of failing electronic circuits or burnt rubber.

Something was approaching from the other side. It wasn't here yet, but in a day, two at the most, it would be. It would break through the wall and then...

What?

Would it lure him into the opening with a siren's call, or would it lumber through the house like King Kong, seeking him out no matter where he hid? Or would it be satisfied to simply grab and devour whoever it first encountered—like his brother or Lauren?

Part of him wanted to pack his shit and get the hell out of Dodge. If he left in time, surely it wouldn't follow him. Would it? Or had it marked him for death—or whatever other unseemly fate the others had met—and would hunt him to the ends of the earth?

He shrugged—he'd stayed here all these years. Why bug out now?

Frank was right. They had to have another little talk with Charlie Benson. Beat the truth out of him if necessary.

25

Joey changed the sheets on his bed after they convinced Lauren Morton to spend the night rather than venture out in the storm. That way they'd be able to get an early start in the morning. The brothers hoped the police chief's presence would encourage Charlie to be more forthcoming.

Lauren put up a token protest, but Joey could tell she wasn't looking forward to braving the storm at night. Not when the house was so toasty warm and the police station was probably as welcoming as a morgue. She could keep in touch on her radio here as well as anywhere. She also didn't take a lot of convincing to use Joey's room, not when the alternative was the living room couch where Joey normally spent his nights, not that he shared that pathetic detail of his life with her.

She bid them good night, a little awkwardly, Joey thought, and retreated upstairs. Joey called after her, saying she could find extra blankets in the hall closet if she got cold. Frank went upstairs after he plugged in the rechargeable battery for the Coleman lantern.

Joey lay in total darkness, listening to the gusts of wind as they came in from the coast, bringing with them more of an apparently endless supply of snow. He briefly considered turning on the TV to see if his favorite weather reporter had any encouraging news about the storm, but he couldn't be bothered to get up and fiddle with the power plugs.

He closed his eyes and tried to clear his mind, but he kept hearing a crunching noise, like a mouse chewing on something. If he opened his eyes, the noise stopped, so he was pretty sure he was imagining it. Imagining an alien being eating its way through the ground beneath him, getting closer and closer to the basement wall with each passing second.

Though the sounds were probably all in his head, he had no doubt this creature—this entity—was doing exactly that. Working its way toward him with a single-minded purpose that made Ahab look like a sports fisherman.

He closed his eyes again and summoned one of his favorite songs, trying to re-create every facet of the music in his mind.

THE DEAD OF WINTER

Every guitar pluck, every synthesizer tone, every hi-hat crash and drum beat. Music filled his head, pushing aside all other thoughts. Slowly, he drifted away toward dreamland.

26

Something touched his shoulder.

He gasped, instantly awake, music dissipating into the ether like it had never existed. "What? What?" he said, voice hoarse, thoughts addled. He was afraid to open his eyes.

"Shhh," the voice said. The hand—if that was what it was—still rested on his shoulder. He could feel the presence looming closer, even though his eyes were still firmly shut. "Move over," the voice said.

Lauren! He inhaled deeply, his first breath in what felt like a minute, and he could smell her distinctive scent in that breath. Cold air buffeted his body as his blankets were lifted. Her weight settled on the sofa cushion, jostling him gently as she crawled in next to him.

"Hold me," she said, squirming around until they were spooning. She took his left arm and clutched it against her chest so he could feel every breath she took. Her body pressed firmly against his. His legs curled up against her thighs and his nose nestled into her auburn curls. After being wrapped up in heavy snow gear most of the day, she smelled of sweat, but it was a heady, intoxicating aroma.

He felt himself getting hard again and tried to ease away from her rear end, but there was nowhere to go. She didn't react to this new development, just continued to hold his hand between her ample breasts. Her breathing slowed and steadied. Her mouth popped open and she started to snore gently.

Just as well, Joey thought. In horror movies, having sex usually meant the character would soon face a horrible death. He'd be impaled by a spike or get his hands stuck in a stump grinder or fall through a plate glass window, severing his jugular and, perhaps, losing an eye for good measure. He took another deep breath, filling up on Lauren Morton's intoxicating aroma. He remembered how she used to look, back when she was a cheerleader, and how she looked now. Then she had been pretty; now she was beautiful.

Yesterday, she'd been a virtual stranger. Today she was wrapped up in his arms.

Wasn't life funny?

With pleasant thoughts filling his head, Joey drifted off to sleep. If he had dreams, he didn't remember them in the morning.

27

The chief of police of Bayport, Rhode Island was still in his arms when Joey awoke. It was dark in the living room, but there was no question she was still there. Her body heat felt like a miniature blast furnace. A soft, pliant blast furnace.

She was facing him now. He was on his back and her head was nestled on his shoulder. Her hair felt like silk on his bare skin. Her hand was planted in the middle of his chest. His right arm was trapped beneath her and had lost all sensation, except for some occasionally painful tingles, like needles being poked into the muscles.

She didn't seem to be wearing much, something he hadn't fully appreciated when she'd joined him several hours earlier. Bra and panties, that was it, so far as he could tell. Not that he was overburdened with clothing, either, having stripped down to his briefs before crawling under the blankets. Said briefs were feeling a little tight at the moment.

Lauren stirred, shifted slightly. Even in the dark, he could feel her looking at him. "Hey, you," she said in a hoarse whisper.

"Hey, yourself," he said. "Did you sleep?"

"Did I?" she said. "Better than in forever." Her lips brushed his cheek. "Thank you."

She moved again and her hand slipped lower, brushing against his erection, though whether by accident or design he didn't know. She withdrew her hand quickly. "Oops," she said, then giggled. "Is that for me?"

A flush of heat swept across his face. "Well," he said, keeping his voice low. "It's because of you."

She kissed him on the cheek again. "Mmm," she said. "That's nice." Her hand returned to his groin, slipped under the waistband of his briefs, and started to stroke him gently. It was all Joey could do to keep from coming right then and there. Who cared what horrible fate might lie in the future if he succumbed in this moment? It would be worth it.

THE DEAD OF WINTER

She twisted her head so their lips could meet. Joey thought about the way she had kissed him yesterday for luck before he went into the tunnel. This was so much better. His warped mind made him think there was another, more inviting, tunnel close at hand, but he pushed that image away and concentrated on the kiss and the way she was caressing him.

An instant after their tongues touched for the first time, something squeaked, a noise with which Joey was very familiar. He knew how every step in the house sounded and how to navigate them to get downstairs without waking his parents.

"You guys up?" Frank called. Another creak as he descended to the second step.

Lauren gasped, relinquished her hold on Joey and scrambled off the sofa, taking most of the blankets with her. She paused long enough to kiss Joey again. "To be continued," she whispered before she planted herself in an armchair and bundled herself up in blankets.

"I'm trying to get your brother to wake up," she said in a loud whisper. "I can't figure out how to make anything work and I need coffee."

"Okay," Frank said. "I'll be down in a few minutes to throw a bucket of snow on him. He was always hard to get up in the morning." The top step creaked again as he returned upstairs.

Lauren giggled, a sound that made Joey feel wonderful inside. "Busted," he said.

"Not *so* hard to get up in the morning," she whispered. She dropped all but one of the blankets back on the couch and bent over for another smooch. Joey put his hand out to caress her shoulder and accidentally ended up with a handful of breast. A mighty nice breast from the feel of it. He rubbed a thumb across the surface of her bra where he thought her nipple was located.

"Naughty boy," she said, inhaling sharply, but she didn't pull away either. "Later," she said, licking his upper lip before dashing upstairs, wrapped in the sheet she'd stolen from him.

28

By the time Frank came downstairs, Joey was up and dressed. He put on a pot of coffee and set about cleaning the dishes from last night's supper. He was still in a bit of a dream state from his definitely-the-opposite-of-a-rude awakening, and more than a little turned on. He had to get his head back in the game, he told himself. Get through this day, find out what they were up against. Slay the dragon.

Then he'd have time for the damsel, assuming the dragon didn't slay him first. Slay all of them.

Frank started working on breakfast. "I think she's sweet on you," he said as he cracked an egg on the rim of the frying pan Joey had just scoured clean.

"Who says that any more?" Joey said.

"I'm serious," he said. "You're all she talked about while you were gone. Down that tunnel. She wanted to know everything about you. Said Patty told her you were funny. And she thought you were terribly brave to go into that tunnel on your own like that."

Joey put the last clean dish in the strainer to drip dry. "No one else could do it."

"Still," Frank said. "I think you might have a chance there if you play your cards right."

"Noted," Joey said.

They heard footsteps on the stairs and turned to look. In the unnatural glow of the Coleman lantern illuminating the living room, Joey watched Lauren descend. She had on her BPD uniform and a mysterious smile, the kind that said she knew something no one else did.

"How'd you sleep?" Frank asked as he turned the strips of bacon sputtering in the frying pan.

She shrugged. "Oh, you know. Strange bed and all that. Can't complain." Joey noted that she didn't look at him as she said this.

"I know what you mean," Frank said. "I'm still not used to being back in this old place. My old room—it's almost like I never left."

"Want some coffee?" Joey asked, hoping he sounded casual.

"Sure. I'd kill for a shower. I must smell like...like...like..." She waved one hand in the air, groping for an analogy.

"Like you haven't had a shower today?" Joey said. Other responses flitted through his mind about the way she smelled, but he intercepted them before they reached his mouth.

"Exactly. Boy, do I need that coffee," she said.

Joey spooned a teaspoon of sugar into a mug and filled it for her. She seemed startled that he remembered how she took it, but smiled as she accepted the mug. Their fingers touched briefly. A static spark leapt between them. The crackling sound was remarkably loud.

Lauren jumped back, but managed to avoid spilling her drink. "Ow!"

"Ow is right," Joey said. He looked at her feet—she was in her socks. The trip across the living room carpet had generated an impressive static charge.

"Breakfast's ready when you two are done exchanging sparks," Frank said.

Lauren frowned at Joey, but he shook his head a few degrees to let her know that his brother didn't know how they'd spent the night.

As they ate, Lauren asked, "So, what's the plan?"

"Head out to Charlie's place. Grill him like he's a murder suspect," Frank said. "That's where you come in. Turn the screws with all the power of your office. Get him to confess."

"Then what?"

"Depends on what he tells us."

She looked at Joey. "I could put you in protective custody. Lock you in a cell."

"Won't stop it from burrowing through the wall or the floor in the middle of night," Joey said.

"Boy. Aren't you a pessimist?"

"Let's face this fucker and take it down. Put an end to it."

"Or die trying?" she asked.

Not normally the most perceptive man on the planet, Joey could see the concern on her face. "Not today," he said. "This is not a good day to die. So I won't. That's all there is to it."

"Yippee-ki-yay, motherfucker," Frank said.

"That's what I'm talking about," Joey said.

29

They plugged the other rechargeable battery in and topped off the gas tanks and the jerry can before setting off for Charlie Benson's place. Lauren took the lead again on her sleek Yamaha with its cool blue piping, throwing up plumes of snow as she roared through the streets of Bayport.

The plow was out, trying to keep the main thoroughfares open, but it seemed like a losing battle. The snow was still coming down as hard as ever. Joey thought they might never be able to clear it all away. He wondered again about the connection between the storms and the disappearances—did the creature only come out during a blizzard or did its appearance bring the storm? Food for thought as he followed in Lauren Morton's snowy wake.

It was still twilight when they reached Charlie's place. The house looked like it was abandoned, what with the high drifts out front, dark windows and not a whisper of smoke coming from the chimney. The oven had probably burned through whatever fuel it had been fed the previous evening.

Lauren was more cautious in her approach than Joey had been the day before, attacking the snowbank at a gradual angle until she reached the top and then doubling back to descend the other side. Joey followed her path, packing down the snow into a nice navigable trail that would probably be completely covered by the time they left. At the top, he stopped for a moment and pushed his goggles onto his forehead while he got his bearings. He looked north, but the visibility was less than twenty feet and he couldn't see anything that might be the crest of a subterranean dome.

They congregated outside the front door and stormed the place like a SWAT team, hoping to take Charlie by surprise and disorient him. They kept their weapons holstered or tucked into their waistbands.

They burst through the outer room, Lauren in the lead with her highly visible and well labeled flak jacket. They didn't expect any resistance, but they weren't taking any chances. She threw the second door open, looked over her shoulder and pinched her nose before rushing into the inner sanctum. Joey and Frank followed on her heels, scattering cats every which way. One made a beeline for the still-open front door but as soon as it saw the mountain of snow outside, it screeched to a halt and sauntered back inside as if leaving the house had never been a consideration.

Charlie was still in bed, lying on his back, a mountain in his own right beneath a heap of blankets and cats. The small room was cool, but not cold.

"Charlie," Lauren said in a sharp voice. "Charlie Benson. Police. We need to speak to you."

It took them a good ten minutes to establish contact with the man, who appeared to be still drunk. Joey started a fire in the woodstove, using a pile of yellowed newspapers and a bunch of sticks and branches that looked like they'd been gathered from the forest.

THE DEAD OF WINTER

Even when they had him sitting up and working on a glass of water, it wasn't clear that Charlie had any idea who his visitors were, where he was, or indeed who he was. His eyes were bloodshot, and his few strands of hair scattered like Red Skelton's. An unholy miasma rolled off him, made worse every time he exhaled. He reeled from side to side on the wooden chair as if he were riding out rough weather on high seas.

"If he pukes, I'm out of here," Lauren whispered to Frank, who was trying to get the man to drink more water.

Frank waved her quiet. "Charlie? It's Frank Shaw. Remember me?"

Charlie's head drooped forward and his shoulders slouched. His lower lip opened and a thread of drool leaked from his mouth. "What? Who?" he said and belched.

Joey put a hand over his mouth and nose. He was starting to feel queasy himself.

"It's Frank. Frank Shaw?"

Charlie head rocked back and forth. It could have been assent or some kind of spasm—it was impossible to tell.

"We were here yesterday?" Everything Frank said to him was inflected like a question.

Charlie's head sagged. Joey couldn't imagine what it must be like inside the man's cranium right now.

"We wanted to ask you what you know about the swamp?"

A bubble formed on Charlie's lips, and then another. He looked up for a second, squinting across the table. "Daddy? That you? Did you bring me something good to eat?"

Frank leaned forward, trying to establish solid eye contact. "No, Charlie. It's Frank Shaw. Not your father. I think he's been gone for a long time." He turned to Joey with a question on his face. Joey didn't know anything about Charlie's father, who would have to be over ninety if still alive.

Charlie set his lip and shook his head like a stubborn child. "He brings me food. When it's stormy."

"He does?"

Charlie nodded. "Still have some." His eyes wandered to the ancient icebox.

Joey pushed a cat aside with his foot, squeezed past Lauren and his brother and went to the fridge. The door had a spring-loaded pull handle like a one-armed bandit that was sticky with age. He managed to get it open without smashing his knuckles.

On the top shelf, on a plastic plate, was a slab of red meat the size of a fist. It didn't look like any cut of steak Joey'd ever seen before. Were there moose around at this time of year, he wondered. Or maybe it was seal meat. Please, God, he murmured, let it be one of those. He pulled the plate out. There was a pool of runny red liquid at the base of the meat. He stood with his back to Charlie and showed the plate and its contents to his brother and Lauren.

Lauren's eyes widened and her face went pale. "Is that...?" she whispered.

Joey shrugged and frowned.

"When did your daddy bring this, Charlie?" Frank asked.

Charlie shrugged. "Last night. Night before, maybe. He always comes when it storms."

"Where does he live?"

Another shrug. "Swamp."

"He lives in the swamp?"

Charlie nodded. He looked at the plate in Joey's hands and licked his lips. "Gonna fry some of that for breakfast."

Joey's stomach lurched. He was about to thrust the plate back into the fridge and slam the door when Lauren placed a hand on his arm.

"Evidence," she said in a low voice. "We're going to have to take that with us." She searched her parka pockets and produced a gallon-sized plastic Ziploc bag with an official-looking BPD sticker on the side.

Joey shoved the meat into it, plate, juice and all. Then he took the bag outside and planted it in the snowbank near his Arctic Cat. He hoped no wild animal would come along and steal the evidence—except part of him sorta did.

It took the better part of an hour to extract Charlie's story a bit at a time, and by the end of it they weren't sure they'd gotten it all. While Frank and Lauren double-teamed Charlie with questions, playing bad cop/worse cop, Joey did what little background research he could on his cell phone. The signal was probably spotty out here at the best of times, but with the weakened cell towers in the area, it was all he could do to perform simple searches. The constant fawning and meowing of the cats that swarmed around him didn't help his concentration.

He *was* able to confirm Frank's suspicion that Charlie's father was long dead, although the circumstances were unclear. Piecing it together from brief news items from the time and Charlie's addled recollections, it seemed the elder Benson had gone missing during a blizzard over fifty years ago, when Charlie was in his late teens. The two of them had

THE DEAD OF WINTER

been out on the swamp, hunting, according to the newspapers, although Charlie couldn't remember what they were after.

"The statute of limitation on poaching expired a long time ago," Lauren told him.

Charlie uttered a feeble, coughing chuckle but would say no more on the subject. The assumption at the time was that the man had fallen through the ice and drowned. His body was never recovered, as far as Joey could ascertain.

"Not dead," Charlie said, repeating his petulant child pout. "He came back to see me. "

"When?"

Charlie shrugged and shook his head.

"Last week? Last month?" More shakes. "Last year? Last winter?" Lauren kept at him until he finally looked up.

"Maybe."

"And he brings you food. Meat. Like that?" Frank said, pointing at the fridge.

Charlie nodded.

"How often?"

"A few times, then he doesn't come for a while."

"In the storm."

Charlie nodded.

"What happened the day he disappeared?" Frank asked. "You were there."

"Can I get a drink?" His face was crimson, as if he was on the verge of a heart attack.

Joey filled the glass with water from the sink. Charlie just stared at it when Joey set it in front of him. "You can have something stronger when you've answered all our questions," he said.

"Maybe we should take him down to the station," Lauren said, making as if to stand, scattering cats every which way. "A few nights in a cell might improve his memory."

Charlie's head whipped back and forth. "Don't do that." He looked at Frank. "Don't let her do that to me."

"Tell us what we want to know," Frank said.

Charlie stared at the water glass for at least thirty seconds. "Not supposed to say."

Lauren settled back in her chair. "Not supposed to say what?"

"About the cave."

For a moment, everyone in the room fell silent.

"The cave," Joey said.

"In the swamp," Charlie said.

Joey pulled up one of the pictures he'd taken in the domed cavern at the end of the tunnel. "This cave?"

Charlie peered at the cell phone screen for several seconds. He raised his bloodshot eyes to Joey's face. "You been there, too?"

"Wait a minute." Frank grabbed the phone from his brother's hand. "You can see this?"

Charlie stared at Frank as if he'd suddenly sprouted horns. He shrugged and nodded. Frank looked at the display and showed Lauren, who shook her head.

"Still nothing?" Joey asked.

"Black as molasses," Frank said.

Joey flipped through the images, sticking the camera in front of Charlie's face each time.

"Those weren't there," Charlie said.

"The tunnels," Joey said, for Lauren and Frank's benefit.

"But this was?" He showed Charlie a picture of the chalk-outlined hole in the floor.

Charlie nodded, then looked away. "Daddy went down there. Thought maybe there was gold or something at the bottom."

"How did he go down?"

"Rope," Charlie said. "He made me hold on. He was heavy, and then there was a jolt and he wasn't heavy anymore. He yelled at me to get out of there, and then he yelled some more."

"What happened?"

"I got out of there. Like he told me to."

"And you never saw him again?" Lauren asked.

"Sure. Like I told you. He brings me food. Asks me how I'm doing. Asks me if anyone's been mean to me."

"Why does he want to know that, Charlie?" Lauren asked.

Charlie shrugged.

"What do you tell him?"

"I tell him what my day was like, and what I had to drink, and where I went in town."

"And…?"

Charlie looked away. He wiped his mouth with the back of his hand. "I tell him if someone hasn't been very nice. Called me names or was rude."

"Like who, Charlie?"

"Don't remember," Charlie said, rubbing his mouth again. A black cat leapt onto the tabletop, startling everyone, He grabbed it and tossed it onto the floor.

"Was Eddie Jamieson mean to you?" Frank asked. "He could be a real jerk sometimes."

THE DEAD OF WINTER

"Made me spill a whole bottle of wine that time," Charlie said. "On purpose."

"Mr. Thompson, the teacher?"

Charlie warmed to the topic. "He told me I was stupid. I was at the store and I couldn't figure out my money. He was in a hurry. He said, 'Come on, you big, fat oaf. Get a move on.'" His imitation of Thompson's voice was eerily accurate.

"And Donna?"

"Everyone thought she was so nice," Charlie said. "But she always held her nose when she saw me, and told me to get a bath and change my clothes. She was real mean."

"You told your father."

"Uh huh. He said he'd make sure they weren't ever mean to me again. And they weren't. My daddy looks out for me."

"What does he look like?" Lauren asked. "Your dad. The same as before?"

"Oh, no," Charlie said. "I wouldn't have known it was him if he hadn't told me." He closed his eyes and shuddered. He lowered his voice and looked around. "Don't tell him I said this, but he's kind of scary. He's good to me and all, so I like that, but he gives me nightmares."

"Describe him," Lauren said.

"He's real big." Charlie said, extending his arms like wings to demonstrate. "He's covered in fur, and he has big red eyes and so many teeth. And claws like swords."

"Is he bigger than you, Charlie?"

"Oh, yes. He has a big belly covered with hair, and big furry feet. And he doesn't really talk, but I can hear his voice in my head."

"Did you ever ask him where he was for all those years?" Lauren inquired.

"Sure. He said he was down there in that hole at the bottom of the cave and he found some amazing things and learned all sorts of stuff about what the universe was really like, and that one day soon I'd get to go down there and find out everything, too." He frowned. "Except I'm not sure I want to. I don't like the dark, or small places." He considered something. "And I don't want to be scary like him."

They were quiet for a while. A couple of cats jumped onto the table, twirling their tails and meowing to be fed or stroked. Joey wasn't sure whether to feel sorry for Charlie or not. If what they suspected was true, he had been doing something terrible, but he didn't know, did he? That had to count for something.

"And what did I do to you, Charlie?" he asked.

"Huh?"

"The last time your daddy was here, you told him I'd done something to you, didn't you?"

"No," he said and looked away. He picked up the glass of water, but put it down again without drinking any.

"Come on, Charlie. You can tell us. I won't be mad."

Charlie exhaled and inhaled deeply several times. He licked his lips and then wiped them with the back of his hand. "You didn't buy me a drink."

Joey blinked. "When?"

Charlie shrugged. "At Sal's one night. You were with a bunch of other guys. You paid for a round. I was standing right in front of you, hoping you'd buy one for me, too." He stuck out his lip. "But you didn't. You looked right at me."

"I'm sorry, Charlie. I don't remember. I was probably half in the bag by then if I was buying drinks." Joey straightened up. "But do you really think I deserve to die for that?"

It was Charlie's turn to blink. "Golly, no. What do you mean, die?"

"Let me ask you this," Lauren said. "And I want you to think about it real hard."

Charlie nodded.

"You know all those people Frank mentioned? The ones you said were mean to you?"

"Sure."

"What do you think happened to them?"

Charlie shrugged. "Don't know."

"Have you seen any of them lately?"

"Sure, I saw Donna just the other…" He trailed off. "No, that was a while ago."

"Right," Frank said. "They're all gone."

"Gone?"

"Your daddy, or whatever it is that you think is your daddy, took them all away," Joey said. "And I'm next. Tonight, probably."

"But I don't want you to go," Charlie said. "You don't have to, do you?"

"Not sure I have any choice: now that you've sicced dear old Papa on me. And you know what he does with these people? Do you? He—"

"That's enough, Joey," Frank said.

"I'm getting out of here," Joey said. He turned and went outside, bundling up as he went. The wind was howling like a

THE DEAD OF WINTER

hurricane in the front yard, churning the snow and whipping it into small funnel clouds that danced and spun before him. It probably wasn't much below freezing, but the wind chill and the ice pellets made his cheeks smart. Even so, he'd much rather be out here in the storm than inside with that idiot who had unleashed an unnatural force on anyone who'd done him wrong. It was a good thing "daddy" only showed up from time to time, or he would have laid waste to the whole town by now.

He stuck his hands in his parka pockets and kicked at mounds of snow. Were his days truly numbered or did they have a chance to fight off this creature that was coming for him? He wasn't going to simply give up, that was for sure.

30

Frank and Lauren stayed inside for another fifteen or twenty minutes. When they came out, they weren't alone.

"Where does he think he's going?" Joey asked.

"He's an extra set of hands," Frank said. "And eyes. He can see things Lauren and I can't. It might help."

Joey sighed and shook his head. "I'll tell you what'll help. The biggest damn guns we can get our hands on. A bazooka, maybe." He looked at Lauren. "BPD doesn't have a few of those lying around, do they?"

She shook her head.

"Elephant guns?"

"Not much call for those, either," she said.

"We should go to the hunting goods store," Frank said.

Joey nodded. "Now we're talking. Load up on a few boxes of Winchester Magnums, if they have 'em. They're ordinarily out of my price range—they cost a few bucks per bullet—but I think it's worth it to put an end to this scourge."

"And save your neck," Lauren said.

"Damn straight," he said. "I'm quite fond of my neck."

Lauren looked like she was about to say something, but stopped.

"Let's get this show on the road," Joey said. "I'll ride with Lauren to get the guns." He looked at his brother. "You think you can handle this thing?" he asked, nodding at the Arctic Cat. "With Charlie on the back, it'll steer about as well as a tugboat."

"I can manage."

They topped off the gas tanks, then set off toward town. When they reached Pottersville Road, they separated, with Frank hauling his hung-over and oversized passenger toward the house and Lauren branching off toward Goodman's Hunting Supplies.

Joey enjoyed the thrill of riding behind her, with his hands planted firmly on her hips for stability. She was an experienced driver, steering the powerful machine expertly through the heavy snow.

Goodman's was closed up tight and no one had made any recent attempts to clear the lot. Lauren tried to call the owner, but couldn't get through. She pulled out a set of keys and inserted one into the emergency access box near the front entrance after chipping away the ice buildup around it. She withdrew a key and a sheet of laminated paper.

"What's that?" Joey yelled over the howling wind.

"Alarm code," Lauren yelled back.

Joey gave her a thumbs-up to let her know he understood.

She opened the front door and punched the code into the box inside the entrance. The alarm system must have been running on auxiliary power, because the building was otherwise dark and cold.

They headed to the back, where the big guns were located. He checked out the Springfield first and the Ruger, and a Savage 116 Bearhunter, but he homed in on the Mauser M12 because its capacity was four bullets plus one in the chamber compared to three-plus-one for the other rifles. It had a price tag of nearly $2000.

"This one," he said.

The rifles were locked up with links of chain, but the hardware section had a convenient supply of bolt cutters, so that didn't seem to make a whole lot of sense. They liberated three of the rifles and a couple of boxes of ammo.

Joey carried the arsenal out to the snowmobile while Lauren left a note for the owner, along with her card. Joey approached her from behind and wrapped his arms around her. In her bulky parka, she was an armful.

She twisted around and returned the embrace, resting her head on his shoulder. "We're really doing this, aren't we?" she asked. "Preparing to fight some kind of monster."

"I guess so."

"I'm scared."

"Me, too," he said. "You know, you and Frank could go off somewhere and let me handle this. It's not after you. You might get hurt."

THE DEAD OF WINTER

"It's my job to protect and serve," Lauren said.

"I think this is above and beyond the call of duty," Joey said.

Lauren stared at him for a second, unzipped his parka, and then her own. She pushed the jackets open and pulled in tight against him so their bodies were in close contact. He could feel her warmth—even through the layers of clothes—and the supple curves of her body where it made contact with his. He thought he could feel her heart beating, though he couldn't be sure it wasn't his own pounding in his chest. His hands found her hips and pulled her closer.

They stayed like that for a while. When they separated, they kissed. This time it was more passionate than before, with a hint of urgency bordering on desperation.

"When this is all over," Joey said. He was short of breath. With a little encouragement, he was ready to take her right there and then. "Let's get to know each other."

"I'd like that," she said, pulling his jacket closed and zipping the front before fastening her own. "Very much."

Joey stifled a sigh of disappointment. This was the second time in a few hours her winsome body had been snatched from his hands when he was raring to go. He hadn't had a case of blue balls this bad since high school.

On the way out, she reset the alarm, locked the door and returned the key to the lockbox. Then she fired up the snowmobile and they headed back toward Joey's place with their miniature arsenal. Joey's hands rested on her hips, but he longed to set them free to explore the rest of her body.

Get your head in the game, he told himself, for the hundredth time. Remember what happened to those kids in those horror movies.

It didn't make him want her any less.

31

The northeast corner of the basement seemed crowded with the four of them, especially with Charlie Benson's hulking and sulking presence, but they made the best of it. Joey carried the rifles downstairs one at a time and set them up, pushing five cartridges into each. He gave Frank and Lauren five more bullets and stuck several in his pocket, then put the boxes on the floor where they'd be able to get at them if necessary. If they needed more than fifteen shots in these close quarters, though, they were probably fucked. Or, at least, he was. So long as the others didn't become collateral damage.

He wished they'd had time to test fire the guns. He had an idea the recoil might be more than any of them expected. He also gathered his supply of handguns in case they ended up fighting in close quarters. He even brought over the machete he'd noticed hanging over the workbench, the one his father had used to trim the Christmas tree branches in bygone days.

They brought two Coleman lanterns downstairs, one battery operated and the other requiring naphtha gas, and ran an extension cord from the power strip upstairs so they could plug in the worklight for added illumination.

"How long?" Lauren asked. "Can you tell?"

Joey shook his head. "It's close, I think."

Charlie stared at the wall. "Right here. Something's coming."

"That would be your old man," Joey said. "Or a reasonable hand-drawn facsimile." He turned to Lauren. "Ever notice how nobody says that anymore?"

Since they'd skipped breakfast, Frank threw together some sandwiches and grabbed a couple of family-sized bags of chips. We make a very strange family, Joey mused as they stood there staring at a blank wall, munching on food, armed to the teeth, and waiting for something to happen. The only one without a weapon was Charlie. No matter how dire the situation, no one thought it wise to give him anything more lethal than a ham sandwich.

Charlie stood with his head leaning against the cement wall. "Chew, chew, chew," he said. "Getting close."

Joey couldn't shake the notion Charlie knew more than he was saying. He claimed ignorance about what his "daddy" had been doing, but he'd mentioned a monster coming through the snow, biting off people's heads. "I wonder what it would do if I buggered off to Florida," Joey said. "Would it dig a tunnel all the way to the Sunshine State or would it—?"

The wall in front of them exploded as if it had been struck by a cruise missile. Shards of cement as big as Joey's head went flying in every direction. One ricocheted off the ceiling and headed straight for Lauren. Joey leaped at her and pulled her to the ground. The rock passed through her leg and disintegrating into a dozen pieces. She seemed uninjured. And confused.

The chunk the size of a fist that hit his shoulder did not pass through him, however. It struck him solidly, knocking him flat.

THE DEAD OF WINTER

"What the hell is happening?" Frank yelled.

Lauren scrambled to her feet and brought the Mauser to her shoulder. "Tell me where to aim," she shouted.

Joey struggled upright. His shoulder hurt like a bastard. Concrete dust clouded the air, making it nearly impossible to see. Something enormous faded in and out of sight as the worklight swung back and forth from the nail that they'd hung it from.

"There," he said pointing

Lauren took aim, but Charlie lumbered in front of her, blocking her shot. Frank drifted to his right, trying to figure out what he should be shooting at.

"Daddy?" Charlie said, extending his arms toward the creature.

As the dust started to settle, Joey saw it for the first time. It was more terrible than anything he'd imagined. It had a face, of sorts, but it was skewed out of all natural proportion. Two black disks with crimson coals burning at the centers approximated eyes, but one was larger than the other and they were uneven on its face. There was a gaping hole that might have been a nose, but it was recessed rather than sticking out, and yellowish orange tentacles writhed within.

It was covered with something, but Joey didn't think it could be called hair—every strand seemed alive. Its arms were as thick as telephone poles, and they ended in "hands" that gleamed in the light, with bladelike phalanges, so many more than ten in total, undulated as if seeking out targets. Worst of all was the crater that occupied the lower half of its enormous head. One moment it looked like it contained more teeth than a prehistoric shark; the next it looked like a gaping maw that could suck anything nearby inside.

Charlie's presence seemed to take it by surprise, but it swatted the simpering man aside like a scarecrow, slamming him against Joey's brother. The two men tumbled into a heap. That cleared the way for Lauren to take a shot. The rifle's percussion sounded like a cannon in the small basement, and the recoil drove her back into the furnace. "Motherfucker, that hurts," she said.

Her shot went wide by about six inches, creating a new crater in the basement wall.

The monster—there was no other word for it—didn't flinch. With Charlie out of the way, it set its sights on its intended victim. Joey raised the rifle and tightened his finger on the trigger, targeting one of the glowing eyes.

"No!" Charlie charged at him like a bull, knocking the rifle barrel askew. Joey's bullet took out the gas lantern, starting a small fire. The rifle clattered from his hands and Charlie's enormous, noxious body pinned him to the ground.

The beast leaned over and grabbed Charlie, wrapping one enormous hand around his body the way a child would pick up an action figure. It tossed Charlie aside and moved toward Joey, who tried to scramble away.

Another deafening report filled the room. This time the shot came from Frank's rifle. Joey stared at the creature, sure Frank's aim had been true, but he saw a puff of dust where the projectile ricocheted off the entrance to the tunnel. A terrible truth dawned on him in that moment. Frank and Lauren weren't going to be able to injure this thing. It operated on a different plane of existence from them.

"Did I get it?" Frank yelled.

The gleaming hand extended toward Joey, who curled into a ball, trying to turn himself into as small a target as possible. "Get out of here, you two. Run while you can."

"Where is it?" Lauren screamed, swinging her rifle barrel left and right.

Joey had no idea where his rifle was, and he couldn't afford the time to get at one of his pistols. He grabbed a piece of cement from the floor and hurled it at the creature.

Lauren, standing a couple of feet to his left, followed the direction of this throw with her barrel, though she probably couldn't see the projectile itself. She steadied her stance and fired again.

Her second bullet—Joey was terribly aware of how few rounds each rifle held—passed through the creature and continued down the tunnel. He didn't have the heart to tell her she was wasting ammo. "Good one," he yelled.

One more step forward and the monster was upon him. It reached out one of its telephone pole arms and caught Joey in an iron grip. The multitude of gleaming, wicked blades surrounded him like a steel cage. The smell was almost enough to knock him out, an overwhelming cloud of putrescence. The hand closed around him, threatening to squeeze all life from him. He couldn't draw breath to scream. Everything seemed hyper-real, the way it did when he was on acid. The lights were brighter, the sounds crisper and the smells overwhelming. This is what it's like to die, he thought.

The creature started to retreat toward the gaping hole in the basement wall. It held Joey out in front of it, as if to ward

THE DEAD OF WINTER

off his brother and Lauren. Apparently it was aware of them, even if they couldn't see it.

He saw something moving on the floor. Charlie, obviously badly injured from being flung at the wall, was crawling toward the hole. Joey knew that if the monster made it back to its lair, he was done. Lauren and Frank wouldn't be able to pursue it, and Charlie wasn't going to be of any use. What fate lay ahead for him if he was yanked behind the basement wall and down into that black pit in the domed cavern? Prolonged torture? Vivisection? Was he destined to become another slab of meat in Charlie's fridge? None of that sounded like a future he wanted to experience.

He summoned every last ounce of remaining strength, found Lauren's eyes, and managed to utter two words. Perhaps his last on this earth or any other.

"Shoot me."

32

Joey closed his eyes and waited for the shot that would put him out of his misery. If Lauren couldn't bear to do it, maybe his brother would show him the mercy of doing so. After all the shit Frank had put him through when they were kids, it was the least he could do.

He felt a shudder and a lurch, and suddenly he was tumbling to the ground. He tried to tuck into a ball, but his collision with the cement floor took the wind out of him. He rolled onto his back and tried to spring to his feet, but his strength failed him.

When he finally got up, he couldn't believe what he was seeing. Charlie was wailing at the monster with the Christmas tree machete, hacking bits and pieces off like a madman. The creature howled in pain, stumbling, losing its footing, dropping to a knee. The embers in its mismatched eyes glowed bright, as if stoked by an arcane wind.

Sparks leapt from its body at each strike, and the room filled with that familiar, nauseating smell of frying electronics. A pulse of energy emanated from the creature and, in the aftermath, it suddenly seemed more present—as if some previously undetected veil had fallen from it.

Enraged, it lashed out with its left hand, all of its innumerable, bladelike digits extended, and pierced Charlie from head to toe. Something changed in the room at that moment, Joey thought. It was like a filter had fallen away from his eyes.

"I see it," Lauren yelled. "I can see it."

"Me, too." Joey heard Frank ratchet another bullet into the chamber and Lauren did the same an instant later.

They could never be sure later whose bullet had gone true—perhaps they both did. The monster's head erupted in a gout of vital fluid as at least one of the projectiles struck it square in the middle of the face. Already faltering on one knee from Charlie's machete attack, the beast trembled and started to fall backwards, toward the hole.

Lauren chambered another round and fired. Frank did the same. They both shot until they were empty, and when they were done, Lauren took out her service pistol and approached the beast, pumping round after round into its torso and head.

It had long ceased movement—the first headshot had probably finished it off—but Joey appreciated her thoroughness.

He stumbled to his feet and groped for his own rifle, but instead he found the machete where Charlie had lost it. He wrapped his fingers around the hilt and approached the prostrate beast. Charlie was still impaled by its hand.

He swung once to sever the creature's wrist, setting Charlie free to tumble to the ground. Joey raised the machete again, feeling for the first time ever his father's spirit beside him, and brought the blade down between the monster's head and its body. He lost count of the number of blows it took. Over and over again he chopped and hacked until the head fell free.

And still he chopped until Lauren grabbed him by the arm, pulled the machete from his hand, dropped it to the ground and drew him into her warm and welcome embrace.

33

All three of them had taken some damage during the altercation. Nothing nearly as grave as what happened to Charlie, of course, but bad enough. Lauren had a dislocated shoulder from the rifle recoil, Frank's left wrist was sprained from where Charlie had landed on him the first time the monster had swatted him aside, and Joey was pretty sure several of his ribs were cracked from where the creature had squeezed him.

THE DEAD OF WINTER

Worse, he couldn't shake the creeping sensation from having been in that thing's grip. Lauren's hug improved matters somewhat, but he was overcome by the urge to strip off his clothes and burn them, then take an hour-long shower.

Before he could do that, though, they had some things to take care of. First of all, they had to put out the small fire still burning around the Coleman lantern.

"Are we sure there's only one of them?" Lauren asked, once that task was accomplished.

Joey circled his nose with his thumb and forefinger. "God, I hope so."

"So we can leave things as they are for now and go upstairs? I don't know about you guys, but I could really use a stiff drink or six."

Frank found a few tattered bedsheets their parents had once used to protect the outdoor plants against frost, which they used to cover the bodies—Charlie's and the other's. A third blanket they tacked up over the hole in the basement wall, which they could now all see. Apparently by attacking the creature, Charlie had done something to impair its ability to cloak itself and any evidence of its existence.

They plodded upstairs, bringing with them the remaining Coleman lantern. Frank grabbed a bottle of scotch from the cabinet and three glasses. They retreated into the living room and collapsed, Frank in their mother's easy chair and Joey and Lauren onto the couch. Frank poured stiff drinks and passed the glasses around.

"To slaying monsters," Frank said. They all tossed the drinks down in a single gulp.

Joey looked at Lauren with admiration "I'm impressed."

"You'd impress me a hell of a lot more if you dug up some of that weed I know you've got stashed around here," she said. "I don't think this hooch is going to cut it. I need to get majorly fucked up."

And so they did. With the cooling bodies of the neighborhood character and an indescribable, im-fucking-possible creature beneath them, they got as high as eagles and laughed themselves silly until they passed out one by one and slept the sleep of the just, or the dead.

Outside, the wind died down and the snow slowed and finally stopped at around noon. The storm—the worst anyone living had ever witnessed—was over at last.

Bruno had left the building.

34

Frank came back to Bayport in June. By then, the last of the snow was gone and the ground had completely thawed out.

Joey and Lauren picked him up at the airport in her police cruiser. It was late on a Friday afternoon and Lauren was about to go off duty for the weekend. She was still on call, but there probably wouldn't be much activity her officers couldn't handle. Bayport was a small town, after all. Nothing much ever happened here.

They went out to dinner at a seafood restaurant before dropping Frank off at his motel. They arranged to pick him up the next morning at ten.

Ever since that wintry night a few months earlier, Joey had been staying at Lauren's place. Her house was small but well appointed. At first, their relationship had raised a few eyebrows around town, but people got used to it soon enough. Joey had been on his best behavior of late, working as a handyman and an Uber driver until something better came along, so everyone decided it was probably a good thing. It occurred to Joey every now and then that this was the second of Frank's former girlfriends he was involved with, but he wasn't complaining. Not one bit.

After packing some of his belongings and taking a delivery from the hardware store several days after the storm, Joey hadn't stayed at their parents' house any longer than it took to check on things from time to time. The store owner didn't ask why he wanted two oversized freezers on his back porch. He was glad of the business.

Charlie fit comfortably in one, after some creative trimming that had put Joey off red meat, possibly forever, with enough room left over for the parts of the beast that wouldn't fit in the other.

Now it was time to dispose of the evidence once and for all. At first they'd considered dragging the remains down the tunnel to the bottomless pit, but on that memorable morning when they'd gotten so high together, they'd decided in a rare moment of lucidity that might be tempting fate. Charlie's father—his real father—had gone into that pit and, as a result, something terrible had been unleashed. They couldn't risk doing the same thing with these remains.

No, they had to be buried, as properly as possible. That afternoon, they had cleaned the mess in the basement with bleach and buried the bodies in a snowbank. Interment to follow in the spring, as winter funeral announcements so often said. Lauren and Joey cleaned the rifles and returned them to the hunting supply store before the owner realized they were missing.

There had been some unease in the community after the blizzard when people noticed Charlie was missing, but it had been a brutal storm and no one was terribly surprised someone had been claimed by it. His body would turn up eventually, everyone was sure.

Working late at night to avoid attracting attention, Joey had sealed the hole in the wall in Donna's apartment building basement before anyone noticed it. Eventually it would heal itself, he believed, but for now, a quick patch job did the trick.

Lauren had the "meat" sample tested privately and confirmed it was from Donna's body. The brothers met with Donna's mother before Frank went back to Houston, expressing their regret they'd gotten nowhere with the investigation. "I'll keep my ears open for anything on the wire," Frank said, and they left it like that. Another open/unsolved case, as far as the rest of the world was concerned.

Now, three months after the battle with the impossible creature, they drove back to the house, the scene of the crime. One of the advantages of not having any close neighbors was that they could work outside without prying eyes. Even though the ground was soft and damp, it took hours to dig two graves near the tree line.

They waited until the sun went down to drag the plastic-wrapped body parts, still frozen solid, into the field, toss them into the hole and fill the graves. For good measure, Joey added a healthy sprinkle of garlic and Lauren surprised them by producing a bottle of holy water. They sealed the deal by planting tiny, inconspicuous crosses nearby. Joey was tempted to piss on the graves, too, but he decided that would be going too far. The old Joey might have done that, but not the new and improved version. Joey 2.0.

Exhausted, they stumbled into the house for one last look around. Frank had agreed with Joey that it was time to sell the place. The real estate market might be soft, but this was a prime piece of property and Joey had been encouraged by a woman at Fitzpatrick Realty who thought she could turn it around for a decent price.

They went down to the basement together, stood in front of the wall and stared.

"You can hardly see it," Lauren said, shining a flashlight on the gray concrete.

"Barely a pinprick," Joey agreed. "Another week or two and it'll be gone altogether," he said. There was a patch nearby where Joey had repaired the hole made by Lauren's first shot, but they had left the mysterious tunnel to close on its own.

"The others, too?" Frank asked.

Joey and Lauren nodded.

"So that's that," Frank said.

"What time's your flight tomorrow?" Lauren asked.

"11:15," he said. "I'll get a cab."

"No way José," Joey said. "We'll pick you up at eight and have breakfast. My treat. How's the Waffle House sound?"

"Sounds good." Frank looked at his brother. "You look good," he said. "Happy."

"Sure am," Joey said. He threw an arm around Lauren and pulled her close.

They dropped him off at his motel and headed home. As Joey pulled into the driveway, Lauren spoke. "Do you think that's the end of it? Whatever was down in that hole—it's gone?"

Joey shrugged. "Until someone else messes with it, I guess. The swamp is getting deeper—global warming and all that—so maybe no one will ever go down there again."

"Let's hope so," she said. "I don't think I could go through that again."

"No shit, Sherlock," Joey said. They held hands as they walked to the front door and let themselves in, making sure to lock the door behind them.

Story Notes

I STARTED "THE Dead of Winter" on January 19, 2015. For no discernable reason, I decided to write the novella by hand in a Moleskine journal. I have written at length before—I have several completed drafts of novels sitting on my hard drive—but always on a computer. Doing it by hand gave me the flexibility to work in a variety of places. Much of the novella was written at the kitchen table or at a nearby bagel café instead of in my home office, always with Brian's tracks playing on my headphones.

At the end of the first week, at the 10,000-word mark, I started the arduous process of transcribing what I'd written into Word. I was a little paranoid that there was no easy way to "back up" the holographic manuscript. If I misplaced the journal, all that work would be gone.

However, instead of typing it in, I decided to dictate it. That was interesting—not only do you have to read the words, you also have to read the punctuation and the paragraph breaks. After a couple of days, I developed a rhythm, especially in dialog-heavy sections where a lot of "open quotes" and "closed quotes" were required. I soon discovered it was better to dictate in a monotone drone, suppressing my instinct to dramatize. I was also intrigued to see what words Cortana had difficulty interpreting. Maybe because of my Canadian accent.

By the beginning of February, I reached the mid-point, averaging 1000 words per day. I hoped I wasn't writing myself into a corner, though, because I didn't have a sense of where the story was headed. I dreamed and thought about it constantly, though, so that at the end of each day's session, I always knew what I'd be writing the following morning.

At about the 2/3 mark, one of the two main characters announced to me that his name was, in fact, Frank and not what I'd been calling him up to that point. I don't think that's ever happened to me before. Search and replace, do your job!

I also discovered that a Tul gel pen is good for about 20,000 words before running dry.

I finished the first draft on February 18, a month after I'd begun and right at my target word count. Of course, the manuscript was littered with transcription errors, so I had to go through it a few times to properly format it and clean it up. But by then I had a pretty solid near-final draft. I sent it to Tod Clark, who graciously agreed to be my first reader. He made some helpful suggestions and was effusive in his support for my story, remaining so in the intervening years while Brian was working on his part of this book.

In addition to the mood set by Brian's play list, I was inspired to a certain extent by the opening line of Hunter S. Thompson's *Fear and Loathing in Las Vegas*. I wanted to start with a character who was high on drugs when weird things happen. Having grown up in eastern Canada, I also wanted to write about the claustrophobia you feel when you're snowed in for days at a time. There's also an element of the "prodigal son," except I wanted to turn that around a little. And, finally, I was inspired by a couple of brothers who I read about obsessively when I was ten or eleven—I'll leave it to you to decide who they are!

The funny thing about writing with music playing is that it permeates your senses in a subconscious way. I don't think anyone will be able to draw a straight line between Brian's mix tape and this novella. They're vastly different in tone and feel. But there's an energy to the story that was supplied by his choice of songs for me and, I like to think, a prevailing mood of dread.

If you'd like to recreate the experience, check out my website for a link to the Spotify playlist Brian supplied to me (I'm old-school—I sent him a CD!). You can listen to his chosen tracks over and over while you bundle up and meet "The Dead of Winter."

The Motel at the End of the World

Brian Keene

For Jeff Burk and Christoph Paul

IT SOUNDS FUNNY when I write it out like this, but the whole damned thing—the end of the world and everything that's happening—all started with the Berenstein Bears.
Or, the Berenstain Bears, if that's how you remember them.
Of course, everybody remembers the Berenstain/Berenstein Bears—a family of anthropomorphic grizzly bears from a series of children's books, right? I mean, come on. There's like three-hundred books featuring them, as well as cartoons, movies, toys, lunchboxes, stuffed animals, and all kinds of other merchandising tie-ins. We all know who the Berenstain Bears are. Remembering them isn't the problem.
The problem is remembering how they are spelled.
Alicia remembers them as Berenstein, same as me. BerenstEin, with an 'Ei'. I'll bet many of you remember them with an "Ei", as well. But if you do a Google search or go to a bookstore or your local library, you'll find out that they're actually spelled with an "Ai". BerenstAin. You might frown in confusion. You might argue, or insist they used to be spelled with an "Ei". But you'll be told that you're misremembering, and that "Ai" is correct.
You'll be told they were always spelled that way.
But this is wrong.
How can it be wrong? That's what you're asking, right? If you're reading this, that is, and God, I hope somebody is reading this. Otherwise, what's the fucking point? Things are getting crazy outside and the world is ending, and I'm spending

what could very well be my last moments hunched over a desk in a cruddy motel room writing this shit down. So yes, I hope that somebody reads it, and if that person reading it is you, then you're probably asking about the Berenstain Bears and how you remember them being spelled with an 'E', and how spelling them with an 'A' is incorrect. And I would agree with you, except it's not. Google image search shows hundreds of book covers, and on all of those covers, Berenstain is spelled with an A. Wikipedia lists the series as spelled with an A, and says the married couple who wrote it spelled their names with an A. If you pull one of the books off your child's shelf, or maybe dig your own nostalgic copies out of storage, they're all spelled with an A.

So, it must have always been Berenstain with an A, right?

But if it was always spelled Berenstain, then why do thousands and thousands of people remember it being spelled with an E?

Here's another one for you. Remember the Bible verse about the lion laying down with the lamb? That's from the Book of Isaiah. It's a famous verse about what happens when Jesus returns to Earth and there's a thousand-year reign of peace or something. I don't know the specifics. I'm not religious. Haven't been for a long time. But my parents were, and they took me to church every Sunday. The preaching and singing were always boring, but I kind of liked Sunday School because we got to color pictures and play games. And I remember, very distinctly, being given a picture of a lion and a lamb to color, and it had that Bible verse printed on it. Isaiah 11:6. "And the lion shall lie down with the lamb".

If you were a church person at some point in your life, then you probably remember that, too, right? If so, then stop reading this for a second. Humor me. Stop what you're doing and go grab a Bible. It doesn't matter what translation. King James, Living Word, Scofield Reference—any of them will do. Once you've got a Bible, open it to the Book of Isaiah, chapter eleven, verse six. I'll do it, too, just to play along.

I just pulled open the dresser drawer and found one of those little Gideon Bibles that seem to be in every hotel and motel in the world. Somebody has drawn pornographic stick figures in the Bible's margins. Seeing two stick figures engaged in a sixty-nine next to John 3:16 made me chuckle, which in turn freaked me out a little bit—because the laughter didn't sound like mine. It was a desperate, uneasy sound.

Anyway...

THE MOTEL AT THE END OF THE WORLD

Okay, I'm on Isaiah, chapter eleven, verse six. Go there. I'll wait for you. Seriously, I'm not kidding. Stop reading this, go find a Bible, and open it up to that chapter and verse.
There. See it? Do you see what I see?
It says wolf now.
It used to say lion.
We all remember that it used to say lion. But now it says wolf.
It has never said lion. It has always said wolf.
Do you see what I see?
Do you know what I know?
If not, I'll tell you. I'll tell you what's going on, because I know the truth. I know about the Berenstain Bears, and Nelson Mandela, and The Empire Strikes Back, and the color chartreuse, and Mister Rogers's theme song, and what Captain Kirk really said on Star Trek, and about spelling dilemma with an 'N', and Scatman Crothers, and Lassie's Rescue Rangers, and Snow White and all the rest. See, I know how they all tie together. I remember correctly. I remember how things used to be. I know about the conspiracy and I'm going to tell you all about it while there's still time.
And you may think I'm crazy, but I'm not.
You know how I know that?
Because you'll remember it, too.

* * *

Do you like those little dots above, there in the middle of the page? I don't know what they're called, but I know writers put those in books, when they want a break in the text. I figured I'd do the same.
Anyway, as I said before, I'm writing this in a motel at the end of the world. Maybe I should start by telling you a little bit about myself.
My name is Dave Giffen. Yes, that's my real name. And before you say it, I've heard all the David Geffen jokes before, so just don't. Just fucking don't. Let me shut that shit down right now. I'm sure my parents didn't plan on me having a similar name to that of a wealthy music mogul. But I've heard those jokes most of my adult life. It's like the scene in that movie *Office Space* when everyone makes fun of the Michael Bolton character because he shares a name with the famous

singer...except now I wonder if that scene still exists. Maybe it's no longer in *Office Space*, or maybe the character isn't named Michael Bolton anymore. That's the problem with what's happening. Things disappear from the timeline. They fall through the cracks and you have to constantly check to see if they are still there, as you remember them.

Shit. Let me start over.

My name is Dave Giffen, and this might very well be my last will and testament—except that the will portion is pretty pointless since I don't have any heirs. My parents are dead, and I don't have any brothers or sisters, or any children. Alicia and I did have a brown cat named Cocoa, but Cocoa is dead now, too. She got killed this morning, back at our apartment, right before we fled. Alicia is here in the motel room with me, so it's not like I'd be able to leave her all my belongings, either. And even if I could, there's not really anything to leave behind or give away. I'm thirty-seven years old, and I've got a mountain of debt; a student loan that I'm still struggling to pay off fifteen years later, repossession notices on a car that doesn't even run because I can't afford to get the starter fixed, shut-off warnings for the utilities and my cell phone—stuff like that. Nobody ever sends me Christmas cards or birthday greetings, but about every other month, I get a letter from the IRS reminding me that I still owe them money on six years' worth of back taxes. Like the song says, I ain't exactly a fortunate one.

Before the end of the world started, I used to daydream about how to get free of all that debt—how to escape and start over again, or better yet, how to fix things so that my bills didn't matter anymore. I'd fantasize about disaster scenarios—an electromagnetic pulse, the eruption of the Yellowstone volcano, a second American civil war, an asteroid strike, the zombie apocalypse—anything that would wipe the slate clean for me. I'd imagine faking my own death, assuming another identity and using that bogus identity's credit line. That's how deep I was in. How deep I'm *still* in. I would never saddle Alicia with that kind of shit. You know what I'm saying? Who could do that to someone they love? Who could leave them stuck with a mountain of debt—something they would never themselves recover from?

Plus, to tell you the truth, now that it really is the apocalypse, those bills are the last thing on my mind. The world is coming to an end. I'm pretty sure the people at the IRS have more important shit to worry about now. All those

THE MOTEL AT THE END OF THE WORLD

fantasies of mine? They're coming true. My prayers were answered. But never in my wildest daydreams or nightmares did I think things would turn out like this.

So, yeah, I think we'll forget all about the last will part and skip right ahead to the testament portion.

This yellow legal pad is Alicia's. So is the red ink pen. The red ink on yellow paper looks very weird in this murky motel light. It makes me think of sickness, somehow, like if you touched the paper or stared at it for too long, you might get some kind of disease. Just looking at it makes me nauseous, which sucks, because Alicia is in the bathroom right now, and there's nowhere else in the motel room for me to throw up. I mean, I guess I could throw up in the little black trashcan that's next to the bed, but then the whole room is going to smell like puke, and things are bad enough already. If the world is ending—and it is, it really is—then I'd rather not spend the apocalypse smelling my own vomit.

Not that this place smells like fucking flowers or Febreze, anyway. Hey, there's another one I just now noticed. Didn't Febreze used to be spelled Febreeze? Or was it always Febreze? I can't be sure. It could be more proof, or it could just be that I'm misremembering. That happens sometimes—misremembering. Not everything is proof of the conspiracy or evidence of the collapse. Sometimes, it's just proof of the fallibility of the human mind.

In any case, this motel room smells like...well, I'm not sure what, exactly. A mixture of old cigarette smoke and mildew and ass, maybe? It's one room, with one bed. A small square box, basically. Not the kind of place where you stay by choice. No, you only get a room like this out of necessity or need. When we walked in the door, the twin bed with a urine-yellow comforter and starchy white sheets was shoved up against one wall, facing a fake cherry-colored dresser. You know the type, right? You can buy them in a box at Walmart and put them together yourself with just a screwdriver and a hammer—if you can read the instructions, that is. Atop the dresser was a low wattage microwave oven whose interior was splattered with the remnants of countless meals from previous guests. A short, black refrigerator—the kind you find in college dormitories—sat next to the dresser. Overhead of these was a tiny flat-screen television, which had been mounted onto the wall. There was also a faded green couch with sagging cushions.

Now, I've moved the couch, the dresser, the refrigerator, and the microwave over against the door, along with a matching faux-cherry nightstand. And I pulled the mattress and boxspring off the bed and leaned them against the window. I can't even begin to tell you how disgusting it was under that bed. The door ain't much, security-wise. Just a dead lock and one of those hook-like bars you can latch it with from the inside. Hopefully, my barricade will stand. I'm grateful the motel room only has one window. There are no windows in the bathroom. Just this one, facing out on the parking lot one floor below. That makes it a little easier to defend. Below the window, there's an air conditioner mounted right into the wall. I kicked it earlier, but it seems to be solidly in place. I don't know if it's bolted into the wall or what, but I don't think it's going anywhere. Which is good, because that means no one can knock it out and get inside.

I can't see the window curtains now, because of the barricade, but like the bedspread, they are urine-yellow, coarse, and thick. When I drew them shut, the fabric felt oily on my fingers. They were filthy and dotted with burn marks. The same goes for the dingy plaster walls and the ceiling. They're also yellow and chipped and there are tiny holes, gouges, and cracks running through them. An old, dusty spider web spans the blades on the broken ceiling fan. Next to that is a dirty smoke detector with a little red light that keeps blinking, indicating it needs a new battery. It's probably going to be a while before that battery gets changed—if ever. At least it's not beeping. I don't think I could deal with that right now.

The only other things in the motel room are my gun, our suitcase—which is full of my notes and research—and the desk I'm writing this at, and the chair that I'm sitting in. The desk matches the rest of the furniture—that same cheap-ass fabricated bullshit. My pistol is sitting on top of it, right next to the notebook. I've got five bullets left, in case any of them get inside. There's also a dirty coffee pot that only holds three cups of coffee, and a flimsy plastic ice bucket that might have the capacity for a half dozen ice cubes, and a couple of paintings on the wall in discount frames. Both of the paintings have pink canvas borders. One shows a lighthouse with seagulls circling it. The other one just shows the seagulls. Maybe the lighthouse vanished in the second painting. Maybe it existed in the painting at one time, and then everyone in the world blinked, and it didn't exist anymore.

THE MOTEL AT THE END OF THE WORLD

That's happening all the time now, here at the end of the world.

Things are here one minute, and everyone remembers them, and then they are gone, and some people still remember them, even though they never existed.

Outside, people are still screaming. I can hear them through the barricade. Earlier, when Alicia and I first got here, they were just jabbering at each other in Spanish. Now, they're screaming in Spanish. I've lived in California almost fifteen years now, but I still haven't picked up any Spanish beyond "gracias" and "si" and a few curse words, so I don't know for sure what they are saying—but I can translate, regardless.

They're saying that they are scared.
They're saying that they are frightened.
They're saying that they don't know what's happening.
But I do.

I used to feel all the things they are feeling—the terror and panic and uncertainty—but not anymore. Now, I just feel... calm. Or maybe resigned is a better word.

Yeah. I feel resigned. At this point, I'm not exactly doing anything about what's happening, but given what the world is up against? Nothing is something worth doing.

The motel is located in the thousand block of Hollywood Way in Burbank, right between Floyd's Barbershop and a printing company. There's a gas station, a convenience store, a Sizzler, and an accountant's office nearby, as well. That's about it for this exciting stretch of Burbank. Alicia and I have eaten at that Sizzler a few times, but I guess we won't be any more. Those days are gone. Everything is coming to an end.

Hell, the street already looks like it's come to an end. The pavement and sidewalks are in dire need of repair. Lots of cracks and potholes. The street is lined with trees—mostly palm, but a few others. I don't know what kind they are. The trees look happy, like that painter guy, Bob Ross, used to say. Happy little trees. But I don't know why they're happy. They shouldn't be. Happy trees are wrong. The trees have as much reason to be afraid as the rest of us do. They did even before the collapse started. It's wildfire season here in California. Last night, they closed the highway down because there was a fire on both sides. As I write this, the Hollywood Hills are glowing orange, and if you go outside, you can smell the smoke in the air. More wildfires are blazing further north. The Napa Valley's had it especially tough this year. I've heard newscasters calling the aftermath and the devastation apocalyptic. But understand something...that shit is nothing compared to what's really happening. The fires are nothing more than a distraction—something for the mainstream media to focus on, so that you don't pay attention to the real end of the world. The collapse? The folding? They can't stop it, the powers that be. The people in charge don't have a fucking clue how to stop it, and even if they did, it's too late now. So, they keep you distracted with celebrity babies and celebrity break-ups and celebrity fashions. They keep you distracted with news from North Korea and the Middle East, and in-depth analysis of what the President said on social media. They keep you distracted with hot button issues like abortion and gun control. Remember when Obama was in office? For eight years, my friends on the Right were adamant that Obama was going to repeal the Second Amendment and take everyone's guns. On his last day in office, I took a picture of my gun safe, with all four of my rifles and all three of my handguns still inside. I posted that picture on social media and said, "He must have forgot to come take these." Now, we've got Trump in charge, and all my friends on the Left are adamant that he's going to outlaw abortion. And I goddamned guarantee you that on his last day in office, abortion will still be legal.

Except that humanity will never make it to his last day in office. We'll all be gone by then...fallen into the collapse, removed from the timeline, and absorbed just like everything else.

But if we were still around, then abortion would be, too. Just like guns were still around at the end of Obama's term. These things are distractions. They serve one purpose—to get you arguing about them and focused on them so that you don't notice what else is going on.

Hang on. I want to light a cigarette. Smoke them if you've got them. Technically, this is a non-smoking room, but that doesn't matter now.

In the state of California, you can't smoke within twenty feet of a building. Unless you're a wildfire. Then you're allowed to smoke wherever the fuck you want to.

The carpet in this motel room is the color of rust. It makes me sick to my stomach, just looking at it—but when I turn my attention back to this yellow legal pad, the nausea remains. There's not much else to look at, though. The only other things on the desk are a phone book, a room service menu, and a guide to local attractions.

THE MOTEL AT THE END OF THE WORLD

If Alicia wasn't in the bathroom, I'm sure she'd appreciate the fact that I'm writing, rather than using my laptop. She used to complain all the time about my typing keeping her awake, back when I still had dreams about becoming a screenwriter. The sound of my pen scratching across the paper is certainly quieter, but I've got to be honest—it's not nearly as satisfying. Still, beggars can't be choosers.

If it sounds like I'm bitching about Alicia, I don't mean to. Please don't take it that way. I love Alicia. Always have. I don't know that it was love at first sight, necessarily, but it was love by our fourth or fifth date, for sure. We connected on every conceivable level, you know? And not just in bed (although we both agreed we had no troubles in that department). I hate to go back to the Bible again, but there is a passage in First Corinthians chapter thirteen that begins "Love is patient, love is kind." At least, there used to be such a passage. I don't know. Maybe it doesn't exist anymore. Maybe it's been overwritten just like everything else. Maybe it's collapsing along with all the other things swirling down the cosmic drain.

But I'm getting ahead of myself again, aren't I? Okay, let me backtrack.

Love *is* patient and love *is* kind. And Alicia was always super patient with me, and kind to me—even when she didn't need to be. And I tried to be those things for her, as well. I guess I did an okay job. I hope I did. We were together for all these years, so that counts for something. But love is about more than just being patient and kind. Love must also be fearless, and strong, and trustworthy. Love is knowing how your partner takes their coffee, and making it that way for them when they haven't even asked. In our case, I take mine black. Alicia prefers hot tea, rather than coffee, and takes it with a little dollop of milk and two Splendas. Not sugar or any of the other artificial sweeteners. It has to be Splenda or get the fuck out. So, we knew those things about each other because we were in love.

Cultural appreciation is a part of love, as well. We like so many of the same movies and songs and books. If love is a shared Netflix queue, then Alicia is my soulmate. Love is knowing how your partner likes their feet rubbed and doing so while you binge-watch a series together. Love is laughter, and love is conversation. But love is also quiet sometimes. Love is listening. Love is communicating through a shared glance or a knowing look. Love is acceptance of our partner's quirks and foibles and insecurities, and gratitude that they accept our own. Love is calmness. Love is how we feel about our partner, but love is also how our partner makes us feel about ourselves.

Alicia makes me feel pretty goddamn good about myself.

I wasn't joking about her being my soulmate. I genuinely believe this wasn't our first time together. Yes, it was our first time together as Dave and Alicia, but we were together long before that. I think we knew each other many times, throughout eternity. After all, what is the human body composed of? Energy. And energy can never truly be destroyed. It can only be transformed. Transmuted. Changed into something else—another form. That's the first law of thermodynamics. I'll bet you remember this from school. The energy of a closed system must remain constant. It can neither increase nor decrease without interference from outside. The universe itself is a closed system, so the total amount of energy in existence has always been the same. The forms that energy takes, however, are constantly changing. Chemical energy can be transformed into kinetic energy. A spark can create a fire. The energy remains constant. It just takes on a new shape.

With that in mind, consider the chemical bonds between atoms. There is a lasting attraction between atoms, ions, and molecules that allows the formation of chemical compounds. But it goes beyond that. I read this science article a few years ago, right before Alicia and I stumbled across the conspiracy, as a matter of fact. In the article, they talked about how scientists at this large hadron collider in Hellertown, Pennsylvania had discovered that certain atoms and molecules were attracted to each other, beyond the rules of chemical bonds. It was almost as if they were magnetically charged. They'd smash them apart, send them hurtling around this giant fucking machine at unimaginable speeds, and yet invariably, certain ones ended up coming together again, like they recognized each other. Now, atoms and molecules aren't human beings. But human beings are composed of atoms and molecules, right? What if, that feeling we call soulmates, that instant attraction we feel for certain people...what if it's just the atoms that make up our body? What if we are connected to each other throughout time, over and over and over again? It's our energy recognizing other energies and being drawn together. And maybe it's not even a romantic relationship every time. Maybe in one life, it's a kid and their beloved pet, or a tree and a bird who picks that tree to build its nest in, or a stream that—no matter how many times others try to dam or divert it—always finds a way to flow toward a certain rock.

Maybe that's love.

It's definitely me and Alicia.

Love is a chemical bond. Love is two dipoles. It's the intermolecular forces of attraction that ties our energy together, regardless of what current form that energy takes throughout time.

I used to take comfort in the thought that—if something ever happened to Alicia—I'd see her again. I don't know if our consciousness transforms with our energy or not. I guess it's kind of farfetched to believe that our molecules remember shit. But regardless, I always felt better knowing that I'd still recognize Alicia in some way. My atoms would be drawn to her atoms, just as they'd been throughout time—since the start of the Big Bang.

Now, though...I just don't know. Now, everything is ending. Reality is collapsing in on itself. There's no guarantee our energy will be recycled after this. If that black hole in the center of the Milky Way galaxy is slowly consuming everything around it—not just across space but through time, as well—then how would our atoms even escape its gravitational pull? If reality is, in fact, being overwritten, then does that principle apply to the atoms that form us? Yes, energy changes form, but the changes happening now—they are different. Would the collapse enact a different change on us, like everything else is changing?

If the energy of a closed system can neither increase nor decrease without interference from outside, and our universe is a closed system, then what forces from outside our universe are orchestrating the collapse?

Scary, right?

Anyway, back to me and Alicia. We met when we were both seniors in college, but weirdly enough, we didn't meet on campus or in a classroom or even at a party. Nope. We met at work. We were both employed by Globe Data Entry Services at the time. Alicia sat two cubicles down from me, and I noticed her right away. We started talking during a smoke break one day (because back then, you could still smoke in designated areas around here), and we hit it off. We started dating and never stopped. We got married on our four-year anniversary of that first date, and we've been together ever since. Sure, like any married couple, we've had our ups and downs. But for the most part, we were always happy. Always content. The two only real sources of trauma in our relationship—and our lives—were our inability to have a child, and Alicia's mother passing away. And over time, it was those two things that led to the Berenstain/Berenstein discovery, and how we found out about the impending end of the world.

So, I guess that's where I should start. I'll try to tell it in order. If you looked up that Bible passage like I told you to, and you saw that the wolf is now lying down with the lamb, then you may be asking "What the fuck?"

You are now where I was six months ago.

If you haven't looked that Bible verse up yet, and you're still reading this, then you may think I'm crazy.

Allow me to dissuade you of that notion.

Because if I'm crazy, then you are, too.

In movies, the end of the world is always sudden. In real life, it's slow, and you don't even notice it's happening until it's much too late.

Here is how it happened. This is how the world ends...

* * *

My father died when I was nine years old. He was drunk and driving and slammed into the back of a tractor trailer that was stopped at a red light. My mother died my first year of college. She was parked at a red light and got rear-ended by a drunken tractor trailer driver. Yes, it's horrifically ironic. I know that. But you'd be surprised how many people bring that irony up in social settings when they learn this fact about my parents. People are idiots, by and large, and sometimes, when I'm drunk, I'm almost glad that we are hurtling toward extinction, one transformation at a time.

But most days, Alicia keeps me from feeling that way.

I don't remember my father very much. I have pictures, so I know what he looked like, but I can't remember how his voice sounded or how he smelled or how it felt to be hugged by him. All I have is his ghost. Most of my memories of him are vague—the two of us fishing in a pond somewhere, me riding in his truck and him singing along to the radio, him trying to teach me how to play basketball (I wasn't very good, but I remember he was patient and kind about it, and encouraged me regardless), the three of us watching the original *Star Wars* trilogy together, and him reading me Berenstein Bears books

THE MOTEL AT THE END OF THE WORLD

when I was little. My father is faceless in these memories, the way people in dreams are much of the time. Maybe that's because he was so tall, and at nine years old, I was eye-high with his hips. I can remember his belt buckle more than I can his appearance.

And I distinctly remember that Berenstain was spelled Berenstein back then.

And I vividly remember the three of us sitting on the couch, watching *The Empire Strikes Back*, and Darth Vader saying, "Luke, I am your father."

These days, Berenstein is spelled Berenstain and Darth Vader says, "No, I am your father." If you don't believe me, then stop reading and go check it out for yourself. Again, I'll wait.

You back? Okay. Maybe you're asking, "so what?" Maybe you're thinking, "does it really matter how Berenstein is spelled, or what Darth Vader says?" And I agree that yes, these are little things. But they are little things that add up to a terrifying whole. In the grand scheme of things, these little things are important.

My parents loved me. I wasn't abused. They weren't neglectful. Dad worked for the Long Beach Naval shipyard, and if he hadn't died, I guess he still would have up until they closed down. My mother taught at the high school. I had her for ninth grade, which was weird. They always provided for me, kept me safe, made sure I knew that I was loved. They did this even after they were gone. It was their life insurance policies that got me through college and paid for our wedding and allowed Alicia and I to make a down payment on a house. And I miss them, even all these years later. Especially my father. I wish I'd had the chance to know him better, and make more memories together. My mother did a great job, though. She really did.

Until she died.

Earlier, I mentioned our cat, Cocoa. Alicia and I found her outside, prowling the street—a feral little kitten. Alicia felt an immediate and strong connection to her, and I knew right away we'd be adopting her. And we did. We took her to the veterinarian, made sure she didn't have any diseases or parasites. (No to the former, yes to the latter, and those were treated). And she lived a healthy, happy life in our home. Until this morning, when all hell broke loose. In truth, this is the first chance I've really had to reflect on her passing. I'm sad that she died, of course. I loved that fur ball. But Alicia was especially distraught. Even when we were fleeing, driving like crazy down the median strips and breakdown lanes lining the clogged freeways, barreling through the smoke from the wildfires, and barricading ourselves inside this motel room—she was crying for Cocoa.

There's no doubt in my mind that Alicia and Cocoa's molecules were drawn together. Their individual energies knew each other before.

And that makes me think about the dog.

This was maybe five years ago, right after Alicia and I found out that we couldn't have children and just a few weeks before Cocoa came into our lives. We were at the ASPCA, looking at dogs. We'd been thinking about adopting one. I think both of us thought it might help us deal with not having kids. We walked the aisles, looking into the cages. All of the dogs barked or whined or yipped, except for this one. She was a mutt—a mix of Golden retriever and maybe Beagle, and she was beautiful. Majestic, even. She didn't bark or whine or yelp. She simply walked to the door of the cage, and stared at me intently. I stuck my fingers through the bars and she nuzzled me with her cold, wet nose. We stared into each other's eyes—hers wide and deep and black, and mine tearing up. I felt a connection so strong it was like static electricity. I didn't know why. All I knew was that I felt it.

I wanted to adopt her right there and then, but we didn't have the money in our bank account. Alicia agreed that on payday, after our direct deposits both hit, we could come back and get her. And so, four days later, we did just that.

But the dog was no longer there. She'd been put to sleep in the interim.

Put to sleep. I've always hated that euphemism. It's murder. Or maybe euthanasia, if you're the type who considers it more humane to kill an animal than to let it live in the wild or in captivity. Call it whatever the hell you want. Doesn't change the fact that it's fucking murder.

Even though I only knew her for a few minutes, I still think about that dog. I'll be going about my business, and then—BLAM—I'm remembering the dog, and I'm overcome with grief and sadness. I think about her the way I think about my parents. And in doing so, I sometimes wonder if that dog was my mother. I wonder if it was her energy, her atoms and molecules, reborn into this new form. That would explain the connection I felt, and that I believe the dog felt, too. Since then, I've waited for her to return again, in some other form, but she hasn't. She couldn't have been Cocoa. This I know. Cocoa was energy that was connected to Alicia, rather than me.

Six months ago, Alicia's mom died of cancer. It started in her bladder and then spread to her kidneys and urethra and then got into her lymph nodes. The doctors found it when she started pissing blood, and they tried to treat it, but the cancer was aggressive. You know how people say that cancer is a quiet death? Those people are full of shit. Cancer is not quiet. Cancer is loud and obnoxious and barbaric. It consumed Alicia's mother from the inside, hollowing her out and shrinking her down into a husk we barely recognized. Understand, Alicia's parents were always very loving to me. They made me feel like I was a part of their family. Her mother became my mother, after my own mom died. Knowing that, can you understand how hard it was to see her in that hospital bed—a rail-thin, balding scarecrow who slept most of the time, and moaned in pain when she was awake? When she finally died, it was like losing my own mother all over again.

A week after the funeral, Alicia's father abruptly announced that he was selling their house and moving into a retirement community down near San Diego. Alicia was upset by this, but we talked about it, and I told her that maybe it hurt her father too much to stay there. Maybe the house, and the community, were reminders of their time together. Reminders of what he had lost. Maybe the house was haunted for him, not by ghosts, but by memories.

With the house on the market, it fell to us to help her father pack up what he was taking to the old folk's home, and what he was either selling or throwing away. I may not remember my father's face, but I remember that afternoon clear as a fucking bell. Alicia and I were in her old bedroom, going through all of the stuff that her parents had kept—all the nostalgic reminders of the little girl who had slept there the first eighteen years of her life. We were boxing stuff up—Alicia's *My Little Pony* figurines and an assortment of Barbie accessories and the posters on the walls. I moved over to the bookshelf, which was lined with children's books, and young adult novels by Paul Zindel and Judy Blume, and dozens of volumes of *Goosebumps* and *The Baby-Sitters Club*.

I turned to Alicia. "What about these books, babe?"

She walked over to me and sighed. I hugged her from behind, gently squeezing her waist and kissing the top of her head. I still remember how her hair smelled that day—like strawberries.

"I always figured we'd have a little girl of our own, someday, and I could give them to her."

And then she broke into tears.

We'd been trying to get pregnant for a long time at that point. The closest we'd come to success was two years before, when Alicia's period was late, and we took one of those home pregnancy tests. A doctor confirmed its positive status, and we were overjoyed, and told everybody, and started shopping. But then Alicia began getting cramps and started bleeding. The pain radiated up to her shoulder. After an ultrasound, we got the bad news that it was an ectopic pregnancy. They performed surgery on Alicia, and took out her fallopian tube. Afterward, they assured us that her other tube was undamaged, and chances were very good that we could still have a baby. I remember one of the doctors quoting us a sixty-four percent chance, which I always thought was an oddly specific number. Regardless of the percentages, it still hadn't happened. Alicia had sort of given up. It wasn't something she vocalized, but I knew. Cocoa had seemed to fill the void, somewhat. I'd always laughed at those people who compared their pets to children, but Alicia's relationship with Cocoa changed my mind about that.

I held her as she sobbed and shook into my chest, kissing her head and whispering assurances. I wasn't sure if the outpouring of grief was about the pregnancy or her mother or both, but it didn't really matter. All that mattered was that I loved her, and she was in pain. We stood there for a long time, and I did my best to comfort her. Eventually, her tears subsided, and she gently broke the embrace.

"I'm sorry." She sniffed. "I got snot all over your shirt."

"It's okay. Do you...do you want to talk about it?"

"No." Alicia wiped her nose with her hand and then shook her head. "No, I just want to get this finished. I'm tired."

She turned her attention back to the books, staring at them with an odd expression.

"Maybe we should hold onto them," I suggested. "I mean, the doctor's said we still had a chance. And there's always adoption. I know we can't afford it right now, but—"

"That's so weird," she muttered, frowning.

"What?"

She handed one of the books to me. Now it was my turn to frown. I took it from her and glanced at the cover. The book was a copy of *The Berenstain Bears and the Spooky Old Trees*. I grinned.

THE MOTEL AT THE END OF THE WORLD

"Hey, I had this one, too, when I was a kid. My Dad used to read it to me."

"Weren't they spelled differently?"

I glanced back down at the book, and my frown returned. "Yeah, they were. It was an e instead of an a."

Alicia bent over and picked up a handful of hardcovers—*The Berenstain Bears and the Bad Dream*, *The Berenstain Bears' New Baby*, *The Berenstain Bears Bear Scouts*, and *The Berenstain Bears and Mama's New Job*.

"All of them are spelled wrong," she said.

"They can't be."

She turned the covers toward me, frowning. "See? They're all spelled like that. They've got an a instead of an e."

"Maybe your parents got you some cheap knock-offs," I suggested. "Like store brand cola instead of Coke or Pepsi."

"But you remember them being spelled with an e, too."

"Maybe my parents bought me the real ones."

She elbowed me in the ribs. "They aren't bootlegs. Look at the art."

"I guess they're all misprints then?"

Alicia shrugged. "I don't know. It's weird though, right?"

"Yeah." I nodded, turning my attention back to the boxes. "What do you want to do with all these My Pretty Pony figurines?"

She laughed, and I was glad to hear the sound.

"My Little Pony."

"Huh?"

"They're My Little Pony," she corrected me. "You said My Pretty Pony."

"Isn't that what they're called?"

"No." She shook her head. "It's My Little Pony."

"Are you sure?"

"Of course, I'm sure, David. I only played with them every day."

"That's so weird. I could have sworn I remember something called My Pretty Pony. I even remember the commercial jingle."

I pulled out my phone, opened the web browser, and did a quick search. Google told me that My Pretty Pony was a short story by Stephen King. It told me that the franchise had always been called My Little Pony. In short, my memory was wrong.

"You're right," I admitted. "My Little Pony."

Shrugging, I was about to put my phone back in my pocket, when Alicia suggested instead that I look up the Berenstein Bears books instead.

So, I did.

That was the real start of it. That was how we learned about the Mandela Effect, and the conspiracy, and the timeline shifts. That was how we eventually became aware that reality itself was collapsing, and that the center cannot hold.

Do you hear what I hear? Do you know what I know?

* * *

The noise outside has stopped. I don't know if that's a good thing or not. There are no sirens. No screaming. No people at all. I want to peek out the window and see what's happening, but I'm scared. I'm tempted to hide in the bathroom with Alicia, but I need to finish this. I suspect I'm running out of time.

And that's what this is all about.

Time.

Just checked my pack. I'm down to two cigarettes left. Wonder if they'll last until the end of the world?

Hang on.

Okay, now I've only got one cigarette left.

Anyway, like I said at the beginning, everybody remembers the Berenstain Bears, but they remember them as the Berenstein Bears. But as those books in Alicia's old bedroom confirmed, they exist now as the Berenstain Bears. Ai rather than Ei. But if it was always spelled Berenstain, then why do thousands and thousands of people remember it being spelled the other way? Are those thousands of people wrong?

Scientists, behaviorists, and psychiatrists say this is just false memory syndrome—a mental disorder which makes people remember things that never happened. You see it used in childhood sexual abuse cases, the most famous of which is probably that Satanic Panic from back in the eighties, when a childcare professional was falsely accused and tried in court for running a devil-worshipping cult out of the daycare center she operated from her home. The woman was found innocent, but the charges and the coverage that stemmed from the trial— all of which were brought about by false memory syndrome— ruined her life anyway. But here's the thing. While thousands of people across the world may suffer from false memory syndrome, that doesn't mean thousands of people across the world are sharing the *same* false memory. That's ridiculous.

THE MOTEL AT THE END OF THE WORLD

And when you press these so-called professionals on that little fact, they blow it off.

Thousands of people remembering the Berenstein Bears instead of the Berenstain Bears isn't false memory syndrome. Instead, it's something called the Mandela Effect, which is named after former South African leader Nelson Mandela, and the confusion surrounding his death. What confusion? Well, if you check the internet or the history books, you're told that he died in 2013. But hundreds of thousands of people around the world—people from all different walks of life—have vivid memories of him dying in prison in the eighties. And thousands more have memories of him being released from prison in the eighties, but then dying in 1999. Can false memory syndrome account for that?

But the Mandela Effect goes way beyond Nelson Mandela. And even though we are running out of time, I need you to do something for me. This is going to be interactive. Remember earlier when I had you look up the bible verse? We're going to do the same thing again. I'm going to give you some other examples, and you're going to pause and consider each one. And if you don't believe me on any one of them, then stop reading and look them up. Then come back to me. Some of the examples might be dependent on your age. Some might be dependent on other factors, which I'll get to afterward. Regardless, if you don't believe me, look it up. Okay?

Let's play True or False.

The Statue of Liberty is located on Ellis Island. True or False?

The answer is False. The Statue of Liberty is located on Liberty Island. It has always been located on Liberty island, despite the belief by millions of people that it is located on Ellis Island. It has never been located on Ellis Island. Check Wikipedia or any history book, no matter how old.

Ready for another? True or False. In the Disney animated movie *Snow White*, there's a famous line uttered by the queen that goes, "Mirror mirror on the wall."? The answer is False. The queen never says that in the film, despite—again—millions of people quoting it, and the line appearing on tons of merchandise over the years. The line spoken by the queen in the movie is "Magic mirror on the wall."

Spoiler warning. All of these are going to be False. So, let's skip the game and I'll just give you some more examples.

I already told you about *The Empire Strikes Back*, and how Darth Vader doesn't say, "Luke, I am your father." He says,

"No, I am your father." My father was a big Star Wars fan. He saw this movie during its original run, and he used to quote the line at me all the time when I was little. But the line he was quoting was wrong. Again, if you don't believe me, look it up. And while you're at it, if you're a fan of the original trilogy, and you're of a certain age, you might remember C-3PO being entirely gold. But he's not. He has a silver leg. Or a silver arm, depending on which timeline you're from.

But I'm getting ahead of myself...

Here's another one from the movies. In *Forrest Gump*, he never says, "life is like a box of chocolates." If you watch the movie now, he says "life was like a box of chocolates." That's right. "Was" instead of "Is".

The most famous line from *The Silence of the Lambs* is "Hello, Clarice." Except that it isn't, because Hannibal Lecter never says that. Instead he says, "Good morning."

Interview With a Vampire isn't called *Interview With a Vampire*. It's called *Interview With the Vampire*. Even the book's author, Anne Rice, expressed confusion over this. And yet, nobody can explain it.

Brian Keene never wrote a novel called *Dead City*. He wrote *City of the Dead* and *Dead Sea*. But hundreds of people online remember reading a book by him called *Dead City*.

Everybody in America, regardless of their age, knows Mister Rogers of *Mister Rogers Neighborhood*. And we all know the theme song that he used to sing at the beginning each show, when he entered the house and changed his shoes. Sing it along with me now. "It's a beautiful day in the neighborhood." Except that now, he says "It's a beautiful day in this neighborhood." And if you go back and watch reruns, even the ones taped onto VHS cassettes from original airings, he has always said "this" instead of "the".

Curious George never had a tail. It doesn't matter if you distinctly remember reading Curious George books or watching Curious George on TV, and you swear he swung around on his tail. You may remember him having one, but he doesn't have one now. He has never had one.

Do you see what I see?

And speaking of tails, the tip of Pikachu's tail was never black. Take a look at it. Don't even bother with the new *Pokemon* stuff. Go back to the originals. There's no black tip. It's just yellow. Obviously, the entire generation who remembers there being a black stripe is collectively wrong.

THE MOTEL AT THE END OF THE WORLD

Sometimes the Mandela Effect comes and goes. For years, people who grew up in the Seventies fondly remembered a cartoon called *Lassie's Rescue Rangers*. It existed. They remembered the theme song, and the network it aired on. And then, one day, it didn't exist any longer. People searched online for it, and there was no record of the cartoon ever having existed at all. Until one day when it suddenly showed up online again, and had its own Wikipedia page, and home media release.

People who were alive in the nineties remember a genie movie called *Shazaam* that starred the comedian Sinbad. Except that never existed. Instead, it's now a genie movie called *Kazaam* that stars professional athlete Shaq.

A television show called *Sex in The City* doesn't exist anymore. It has never existed. Now it's called *Sex and The City*.

Captain Kirk never said "Beam me up, Scotty" in the original *Star Trek* series. If you don't believe me, look it up. Or better yet, binge-watch the series, if the world hasn't ended yet.

My bologna has a first name. it's O-S-C-A-R. My bologna has a second name, it's..." People older than me insist that the next line in this commercial jingle was 'M-E-Y-E-R". Except that's not how the brand spells it. If you look on the packages of their lunch meats and hot dogs, the bologna is spelled M-A-Y-E-R.

Chick-fil-A is not spelled any of the other ways you remember it being spelled.

Kit Kat candy bars don't have a dash in their name. Neither do Froot Loops. Also, Froot Loops are no longer spelled Fruit Loops.

And while we are on the subject of fruit, if you are of a certain age, you might remember the Fruit-of-the-Loom underwear symbol, which was a cornucopia of fruit. That cornucopia no longer exists and has never existed.

Jiffy brand peanut butter doesn't exist. Something called Jif has taken its place.

There was an old actor named Scatman Crothers who people insist was named Scatman Carruthers.

You know rich Uncle Pennybags from Monopoly? He's never worn a monocle.

The last line Freddie Mercury sings in Queen's "We Are the Champions" is not—and has never been—"...of the world." If you don't believe me, go listen to it.

BRIAN KEENE

Mona Lisa—the woman in that famous painting? She used to have an emotionless expression. Now she's smiling.

For years, people made fun of actress Sally Field, who, when accepting an Oscar award, said to the crowd, "You like me. You really like me!" *Saturday Night Live* even did a sketch about this. I remember watching it with my dad, who had the whole series on DVD and used to explain the references to me. But Sally Field never said that. Instead, she said, "Right now you like me." And the *Saturday Night Live* sketch no longer exists. I went through my father's DVD collection and checked. It's no longer there.

Millions of people swear that the word dilemma used to be spelled with an N, like this—

'dilemna'.

The color chartreuse is a shade between yellow and green, except that about half the population of the world remember it being a shade between red and pink.

The creator of the *Peanuts* cartoon is Charles Schulz, unless you are one of the many who remembers it as Charles Schultz.

Do you see what I see?

* * *

When you're driving to work, do you ever pass by a place, maybe a gas station or a house or a store, and you could swear you've never seen it before? You are positive that it wasn't there the day before?

That's because it wasn't.

But it is now.

And it always has been.

Yesterday, it existed elsewhere. Today, it exists here.

The same thing can happen with people. Maybe once again, during your commute to work, you see somebody that can't possibly be there? Someone who looks like a dead friend or relative? Or maybe you spot a living friend's doppelgänger from across the subway station, but you know logically that it can't be that friend, because they are currently living on the opposite side of the country?

What if it was that person, but not the version you know?

Do you know what I know?

THE MOTEL AT THE END OF THE WORLD

* * *

I could go on listing examples all day, but I'm running out of time. Alicia is still in the bathroom, and the sounds have started outside again. Lots of movement and commotion. I'm fighting the urge to peek out the barricade, because I'm afraid of what I might see.

I'm afraid of what the end might look like.

Hopefully, you've looked up some of my examples. They sparked something inside of you, and you said, "Hey, I remember Darth Vader saying that" and you've now learned otherwise, and you no longer think I'm crazy. So, let me explain to you how this happened.

Earlier, I mentioned the hadron collider in Hellertown, Pennsylvania. They turned it on in 2004, and the world didn't end like people feared it would.

It didn't *end*, but it *started* to end.

One of the things they discovered by using the collider was the Higgs Boson particle—the so-called God Particle. That's the thing that's responsible for all physical forces. It's the glue that holds the universe together. But what they didn't realize was that in 2004, when they discovered the Higgs Boson, they also started everything unraveling.

If you know about quantum physics or string theory, then you know about the scientific possibility that there are alternate universes—mirror images of our Earth and ourselves that exist simultaneously in a different dimension. Shit, you don't have to have studied quantum mechanics to know about that. It's the basis of half the comic books and science fiction movies ever made. All of those alternate realities are held together by the Higgs Boson particle. Think of it as molasses, spread out across space and time, holding everything together with its stickiness. Some occultists and online weirdos call that The Labyrinth, and they say it touches and connects everything.

When they turned on the collider, it ripped a hole in that molasses, and something began bleeding into our universe. Some people say it is dark matter or antimatter. Some say it is something beyond our understanding of physics and the laws of nature—a physical force that our science is not yet advanced enough to explain. Others on the internet say they are monsters—entities known as The Thirteen, who existed beyond space and time, and who have now come to our universe, thanks to the rift. They have names like Ob and Leviathan and Meeble and Shtar. And when they were released back in 2004, they slowly and methodically began destroying realities. That's plural, not singular.

It turns out all three schools of thought are simultaneously correct. And if you think it sounds crazy that antimatter monsters from beyond space and time are chewing their way across the realities, then I'd just ask you this one thing.

It also sounded crazy when I told you about the Berenstain Bears and *The Empire Strikes Back* and all the other stuff—until you looked into it yourself.

So...if I'm crazy? Then you're crazy, too.

By 2012, these entities which our science can't yet explain had done enough damage to the multiverse that the still-unharmed realities began to take notice. People couldn't explain it, but something was wrong. Things weren't as they remembered. They called it the Mandela Effect, which is a nice, catchy name for what is the end of everything. The slow collapse. The great implosion.

Remember the Mayan prophecy that the world would end in 2012? They called it the end of the cycle of creation. Well, it turns out that the Mayan's were right. The worlds really did end in 2012. We just didn't know it.

As everything unravels, all of these alternate realities are collapsing in on one another. We go through our lives unaware of it. And as they collapse, the timelines are merging. Let's say you go to bed with your wife tonight. When you both wake up tomorrow, she may no longer be the wife you remember. Instead, she's a version of herself from another timeline—an alternate reality where some things—little things like the Berenstain Bears or the color chartreuse—are different. Neither of your timelines no longer exist, because they have folded in on each other like a piece of paper. They've merged.

The collapse started in 2012. That's when people began to notice the Mandela Effect. Since then, with each passing year, it's gotten stranger and stranger. And the timeline glitches aren't the only noticeable difference. Wildfires, earthquakes, tsunamis, volcanic eruptions, and other natural disasters are increasing with an alarming frequency. Political, religious, and racial polarization is running high. Violence is on the rise. There are so many mass shootings now that they barely warrant a mention on the news.

The center cannot hold, and things are falling apart.

And so am I.

THE MOTEL AT THE END OF THE WORLD

Alicia and I spent months watching videos online and reading message board posts, studying this conspiracy, and unraveling all the threads. And it is indeed a conspiracy. Our governments know all about it. They're not telling us because there's no way to fucking to stop it. I mean, we can't even land a human being on Mars. You really think we have the capability or a plan for stopping timelines from collapsing in on each other? So they keep it secret and cover everything up. I guess they figure if they were straight with us—if they told us what was really happening—then humanity would collectively lose our shit. But that seems to be happening anyway, right? Like I said, violence is on the rise. Remember when a mass shooting was a big thing, and it dominated all the cable news channels and your social media feed? Now, unless there is a really big body count or unless they can somehow tie it to politics, it gets mentioned for five minutes, and then it's on to the next news story.

People are losing their minds. Depression, anxiety, suicide... all on the rise. And instead of worrying about important shit, we spend our time arguing about pointless distractions. We debate Star Wars and superhero movies and whether or not our favorite pop culture icons are sufficiently "woke" enough. The top one percent are getting wealthier with each passing day, and the rest of us are getting poorer. Our governments and our corporations work hand in hand. It doesn't matter what system you live under. Democracy, communism, socialism—it's all just a big corporate oligarchy. A company like the Globe Corporation has infinitely more power than any world government. In the past, people would have risen up against this shit. They would have said enough is enough. But now? Now, they just stare at their screens, and scroll past it all, and stay pacified and occupied by trivial bullshit.

Because they're scared. They know something is wrong. Even those who don't know about the conspiracy, the ones who think the Mandela Effect is just crazy talk—even they know something is wrong. They might not acknowledge it. They might not even be aware of it, consciously. But deep down inside, in the lizard part of their brain, they know something has changed. Something is different. Something has gone terribly awry and it doesn't seem to be stopping.

Do they see what I see?

Do they know what I know?

And I'm sorry to tell you this, but once your eyes have been opened to what's happening, you can't go back to the way things were before. You'll begin to notice more and more changes. It will always be little things. The title of a book. A line from a movie. The year a celebrity died. The spelling of a word. But those little things matter. Those little things add up, and as they do, you'll begin to feel overwhelmed.

I know I certainly do. I'm tired of things changing. I'm tired of having no control. I'm scared of everything that's happened and I'm scared of what's coming next. My only relief is that I know the fear won't last much longer, because it's the end of the world.

Or at least, the end of this world.

The end of my world.

They're pounding on the door now. It will all be over soon.

Time for that last cigarette.

Okay...

Understand something. What I did to Alicia? It was because I loved her. Yeah, she was upset when we got here to the hotel, and I can only imagine how we must have looked as we ran across the parking lot—Alicia crying and distraught and me practically dragging her behind me with one hand, waving my gun in the other. She was upset about Cocoa, but we'd agreed ahead of time that it wasn't right to let the cat suffer the end alone, after we were gone. Killing Cocoa was the humane thing to do.

What I hadn't counted on was our neighbor hearing the shot and calling the police. And I also hadn't counted on me chickening out. The plan had been Cocoa, then Alicia, and then myself, but when the time came, I couldn't do it. Maybe it's because of the way Alicia was screaming and crying, or maybe it was the sirens and the commotion. But instead of following through, I got us into the car, and we ended up here.

Here in this motel at the end of our world.

After we barricaded the room, and I'd calmed down a bit, I was able to do it. I followed through. And now there's no chance I'll wake up next to a different Alicia tomorrow, and no chance she'll wake up to a different version of me.

Her timeline has ended.

Like Cocoa, it was the humane thing to do.

My pistol is still sitting atop the cheap-ass fabricated desk, and I still have five bullets left.

They're pounding on the door now, and there's a lot of shouting, but I can't understand what they're saying because the buzzing in my head is too loud.

THE MOTEL AT THE END OF THE WORLD

It could be the cops, or it could be those things I mentioned earlier—The Thirteen.

Either way, I'm not crazy. And neither are you.

Unless I am, of course. But if that's true, then you're crazy too, because you were nodding along earlier, and you looked up the examples I gave you.

You see what I see. You know what I know.

I'm going to put down this pen now and pick up the gun.

The door is buckling in the frame.

This is the end.

Story Notes

THIS IS ACTUALLY the second novella that was inspired by Bev's playlist.

The first one, which was called "Rites of Spring" or "Rites of Passage" (I liked both titles and never did pick one over the other) is sitting unfinished on my laptop. It's unfinished because while I was in the middle of writing it, Stephen King released a then-new short story collection called *Just After Sunset*, and I bought it, and read it, and when I got to "N" I smiled and stopped writing my novella because the plots were just way too similar.

This isn't the first time something like that has happened. Years ago, I finished writing a novel called *A Gathering of Crows*. In one of the book's early scenes, a carload of surplus teenagers goes racing down the road and smashes headlong into an invisible barrier that's been placed around the town. I turned the manuscript in to my publisher and bought the then-new Stephen King novel *Under the Dome*, which contains an early scene of an airplane full of surplus characters smashing headlong into an invisible barrier that's been placed around the town.

I'm not exactly a metaphysical guy. But times like those, I wonder if author and occultist Alan Moore might be right regarding 'Ideaspace'—a dimensional space that he theorizes is accessible by creatives and explains why so many things seem to pop into the cultural and entertainment zeitgeist at seemingly the same time.

Either that, or great minds think alike.

Anyway, I told Bev we'd have to hold off until inspiration hit me again, and it took a long time for that to happen. I thought about cheating. I considered finishing just any old novella and saying that Bev's playlist fueled it, but that would have defeated the entire purpose of this artistic exercise. So, I waited.

And waited.
And Bev waited too.
And then this idea struck me.

Knowing that I love a good conspiracy theory, authors and publishers Jeff Burk and Christoph Paul told me about The Mandela Effect. I looked into it, and much like the main character, my mind was blown. I remember what Darth Vader said! I remember that Bible verse! How can they possibly be different now? But they are.

I spent a week going down the Mandela Effect rabbit hole online, and Bev's mix-tape was playing in the background for much of that time, and then...everything finally clicked.

I knew from the beginning that I wanted David to be an unreliable narrator, and I knew that he would die there in that motel room. But I also needed him to be sympathetic. I needed the reader to empathize with him. I wanted examples of things that both he and the reader would remember—examples that the reader could then research themselves. If he's an unreliable narrator, but he's offering examples that the reader can empathize with, then maybe the reader would be kept on their toes, and root for the guy, not knowing that he's already killed his girlfriend and, in fact, just mentally ill. "Dead Man's Blues", from Bev's mix-tape, was the spark of that for me.

I hope that you enjoyed it. But I should warn you, twenty years from now when you come back and re-read it? There will be subtle differences that weren't there before.

About the Authors

BEV VINCENT got a late start at writing, although he dabbled with short stories while at university in the 1980s. In 2001, he became a contributing editor with *Cemetery Dance* magazine, writing "Stephen King: News from the Dead Zone" for each issue. His first book, *The Road to the Dark Tower*, appeared in 2004 and was nominated for a Bram Stoker Award. Barnes & Noble commissioned *The Stephen King Illustrated Companion*, nominated for both an Edgar and a Stoker. His third book, *The Dark Tower Companion*, came out in 2013. In addition to writing hundreds of essays and book reviews for a variety of outlets, Vincent has published over ninety short stories, which have appeared in places like *Ellery Queen's Mystery Magazine, Alfred Hitchcock's Mystery Magazine, Borderlands 5*, several *Shivers* anthologies and two Mystery Writers of America anthologies. He has also contributed stories to *Doctor Who* and *The X-Files* anthologies. Four of his stories are collected in *When the Night Comes Down* and another four in a CD Select eBook. His story "The Bank Job" won the Al Blanchard Award in 2010 and "The Honey Trap" from *Ice Cold* was nominated for an ITW Thriller Award in 2015. His only foray thus far into the world of film was his experience co-writing the script for the Dollar Baby adaptation *Stephen King's Gotham Café*. In 2018, he co-edited *Flight or Fright* with King. This anthology of scary stories about turbulent flights has been translated into French, Dutch, Italian, Russian, Bulgarian, Swedish, Czech, German, Polish, Serbian, Japanese, Spanish, Greek and Korean. Originally from New Brunswick, Canada, Vincent has lived in Texas for over thirty years, twenty-five of them with his wife Mary Anne. His home on the internet is bevvincent.com.

BRIAN KEENE writes novels, comic books, short fiction, and occasional journalism for money. He is the author of over fifty books, mostly in the horror, crime, and dark fantasy genres. His 2003 novel, *The Rising*, is often credited (along with Robert Kirkman's *The Walking Dead* comic and Danny Boyle's *28 Days Later* film) with inspiring pop culture's current interest in zombies. Keene's novels have been translated into German, Spanish, Polish, Italian, French, Taiwanese, and many more. In addition to his own original work, Keene has written for media properties such as *Doctor Who, The X-Files, Hellboy, Masters of the Universe*, and *Superman*. Several of Keene's novels have been developed for film, including *Ghoul, The Ties That Bind*, and *Fast Zombies Suck*. Several more are in-development or under option. Keene also serves as Executive Producer for the independent film studio Drunken Tentacle Productions. Keene also oversees Maelstrom, his own small press publishing imprint specializing in collectible limited editions, via Thunderstorm Books. Keene's work has been praised in such diverse places as *The New York Times, The History Channel, The Howard Stern Show, CNN.com, Publisher's Weekly, Media Bistro, Fangoria Magazine*, and *Rue Morgue Magazine*. He has won numerous awards and honors, including the 2014 World Horror Grandmaster Award, 2001 Bram Stoker Award for Nonfiction, 2003 Bram Stoker Award for First Novel, 2004 Shocker Award for Book of the Year, and Honors from United States Army International Security Assistance Force in Afghanistan and Whiteman A.F.B. (home of the B-2 Stealth Bomber) 509th Logistics Fuels Flight. A prolific public speaker, Keene has delivered talks at conventions, college campuses, theaters, and inside Central Intelligence Agency headquarters in Langley, VA. The father of two sons, Keene lives in rural Pennsylvania.

ONE OF THE FINEST COMING-OF-AGE STORIES OF

THE CURRENT HORROR GENERATION!

GET

CHAD LUTZKE'S
OF FOSTER HOMES AND FLIES

IN **_HARDBACK_** FOR THE FIRST TIME!

"Original, touching coming of age."

—Jack Ketchum,

author of *The Girl Next Door*

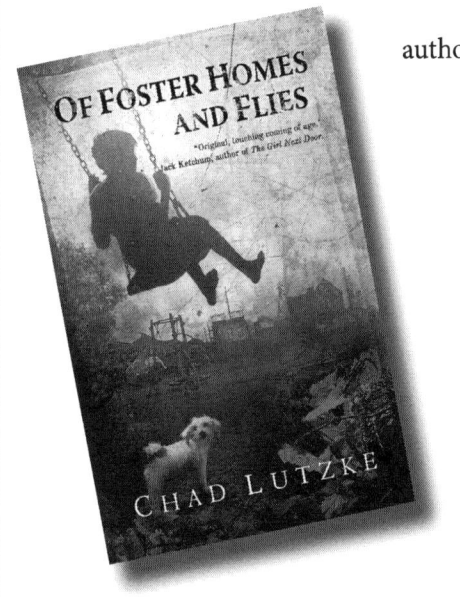

HAYWARD AND FORD JOIN FORCES TO CREATE ONE OF THE YEAR'S MOST ANTICIPATED READS!

GET
ROBERT FORD & MATT HAYWARD'S
A PENNY FOR YOUR THOUGHTS

IN **HARDBACK, PAPERBACK AND EBOOK TODAY**!

"I would recommend to anyone and everyone. This is a must read!"

—Sadie Hartmann, Cemetery Dance

SANGIOVANNI'S AWARD-NOMINATED CLASSIC

RETURNS IN HARDBACK!

GET

MARY SANGIOVANNI'S THE HOLLOWER

IN **<u>HARDBACK</u> TODAY FROM POLTERGEIST PRESS!**

"Mary SanGiovanni is one of my favorite authors. Her work is cause for celebration!"

—Brian Keene, author of *The Rising* and *Ghoul*

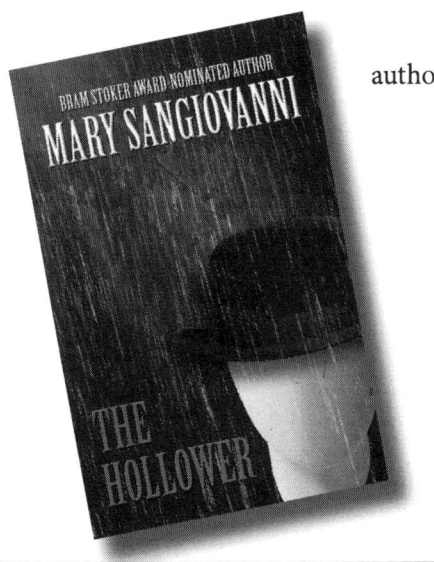

DRIES RETURNS WITH A SPLATTERPUNK EPIC THAT WOULD MAKE DAVID LYNCH TAKE NOTE!

GET

AARON DRIES'S
A PLACE FOR SINNERS

IN **HARDBACK, PAPERBACK AND EBOOK TODAY**!

"...has all the trademarks of a talent bound for the bestseller lists. Remarkable."

—Kealan Patrick Burke, author of *Sour Candy* and *Kin*

A BRAND NEW NOVEL FROM THE AUTHOR OF *WHAT DO MONSTERS FEAR?*

GET

MATT HAYWARD'S THOSE BELOW THE TREE HOUSE

IN **HARDBACK, PAPERBACK AND EBOOK TODAY**!

"A towering epic that blazes with energy, excitement and horror."
—Simon Clark, author of *Blood Crazy*

Made in the USA
Middletown, DE
27 March 2021